Joyce was the dancer to watch

They were all looking at her. The entire class. Tamu. Clarke. J'had. And for the first time it felt wonderful to have so many eyes upon her. Not because her tail was round or because they were waiting to laugh. But because she was the dancer to watch. She didn't want to shrink away from their waiting eyes. Joyce wanted to dance for them.

Once the drumming started, Joyce's imagination let her become anyone she wanted to be. She felt her arms and torso telling the story of the river maiden gathering cascades of water. She moved fluently within the phrases, cleverly scooping water into calabash gourds where the others danced the phrase as a simple arm flutter—not like Joyce the River Maid raising the Volta! Balancing the imaginary gourd on her head, she gave richness to a dry earth and gave dance to a cheering studio.

OTHER PUFFIN BOOKS YOU MAY ENJOY

Charlie Pippin   Candy Dawson Boyd

Chevrolet Saturdays   Candy Dawson Boyd

Fast Sam, Cool Clyde, and Stuff   Walter Dean Myers

Forever Friends   Candy Dawson Boyd

Freedom Songs   Yvette Moore

Growin'   Nikki Grimes

The Hundred Penny Box   Sharon Bell Mathis

An Island Like You   Judith Ortiz Cofer

Just Like Martin   Ossie Davis

Just My Luck   Emily Moore

Learning by Heart   Ronder Thomas Young

Let the Circle Be Unbroken   Mildred D. Taylor

Listen for the Fig Tree   Sharon Bell Mathis

Ludie's Song   Dirlie Herlihy

Marcia   John Steptoe

My Black Me   Arnold Adoff, editor

My Life with Martin Luther King, Jr.   Coretta Scott King

The Road to Memphis   Mildred D. Taylor

Roll of Thunder, Hear My Cry   Mildred D. Taylor

Sidewalk Story   Sharon Bell Mathis

Something to Count On   Emily Moore

Take a Walk in Their Shoes   Glennette Tilley Turner

Teacup Full of Roses   Sharon Bell Mathis

The Young Landlords   Walter Dean Myers

BLUE
TIGHTS

Rita Williams-Garcia

PUFFIN BOOKS

to my mother, Miss Essie,

Grandma Edie,

and Roz, who nurtured;

to Pat, who listened;

and to Pete, who was there

PUFFIN BOOKS
Published by the Penguin Group
Penguin Books USA Inc., 375 Hudson Street, New York, New York 10014, U.S.A.
Penguin Books Ltd, 27 Wrights Lane, London W8 5TZ, England
Penguin Books Australia Ltd, Ringwood, Victoria, Australia
Penguin Books Canada Ltd, 10 Alcorn Avenue, Toronto, Ontario, Canada M4V 3B2
Penguin Books (N.Z.) Ltd, 182-190 Wairau Road, Auckland 10, New Zealand

Penguin Books Ltd, Registered Offices: Harmondsworth, Middlesex, England

First published in the United States of America by
Lodestar Books, E.P. Dutton, 1988
Published in Puffin Books, 1996

10 9 8 7 6 5 4 3 2 1

THE LIBRARY OF CONGRESS HAS CATALOGED THE LODESTAR EDITION AS FOLLOWS:
Williams-Garcia, Rita.
Blue tights.
Summary: Growing up in a city neighborhood, fifteen-year-old Joyce, unsure of
herself and not quite comfortable with her maturing body, tries to find a
place to belong and a way to express herself through dance.
[1. Afro-Americans—Fiction. 2. Self-confidence—Fiction.
3. Dancing—Fiction. 4. City and town life—Fiction.]
I. Title.
PZ7.W6713Bl 1987 [Fic] 87-17156
ISBN 0-525-67234-6

Puffin Books ISBN 0-14-038045-0
Printed in the United States of America

❧ One

The 2:15 Special was pulling in alongside Mays department store on Jamaica Avenue twelve seconds short of all hell spilling over. The windows were heavily frosted from the panting mouths of some eighty-odd high schoolers crammed in the seats and aisles, making human pyramids. When there was no more air to breathe in, let alone space to turn around in, confetti scraps from an unclaimed loose-leaf showered the back end of the Special.

Stereo warfare blared and thumped between a Sony and a lesser brand. Salsa versus funk. A thundering herd of orange-and-blue clad boosters with jingles and mini pom-poms dangling from sneakers dominated with a traditional threat: *Boom boom! Stomp Bayside!*

It was coming. The bus driver's revenge. Payback for the stereo warfare, the cackling, the fist-ups, and the dust bomb from herb and menthol cigarettes. At the last second the high schoolers prepared themselves for the abrupt halt against the curb. All except for—bangsplat!!—Joyce, who just wasn't swift enough.

Joyce landed backside first with half of Cardozo High looking down at her. Even worse, Cindi and Jay-Jay

1

were looking down at her from their boyfriends' laps. If Joyce had had a boyfriend's lap to sit on, none of this would have happened. Joyce rubbed her side, acknowledging that fact, and blamed the driver for pointing it out to the world.

The driver shook his head at their raging adolescence, showing disgust at the sight of Joyce, who was practically at his feet.

Oh yeah? What you lookin' at? was clearly scowled on her delicate, round face.

Using her weight and oversized dance bag, Joyce Collins picked herself up and fought her way through the other Cardozoans who pushed back just for the sake of pushing. Cindi and Jay-Jay avoided the pushing by getting off the bus fast. Meanwhile, Melvyn and Marvin started up their usual antics, which included rushing the crowd from the rear and sneaking through some girl's legs. They plain old had no sense. Blame it on the football team's off season, one, or their mama, two, for not teaching them any better. In their mad shoving the Davis twins made the mistake of pushing up against Joyce's behind. Now why did they do that? They knew why, and stood there grinning, the yellow siamese piglets in orange-and-blue letterman jackets. Stood there grinning and daring Joyce, knowing she enjoyed it despite her usual protests and empty threats. Joyce elbowed Marvin's side without considering any of his 185 pounds and nicked his head with *Biology: A Life Science*. Let them know she was in no mood.

Some white lady—probably someone's granny—made the mistake of getting on the Special and cast obvious looks of disdain. In return she got Joyce's tossed head and rolling eyes, indicating that this was just part of the regular goings-on at 2:45, and she should just keep on knitting.

The Dean of Girls, Mr. Weiner's class, the honors classes, plus Ms. Sobol and her precious *Sleeping Beauty* contributed to Joyce's unleashed tension as she hit the streets at 2:45 every Monday through Friday. This time, keeping the salty cuss in her mouth, Joyce let the bus driver off with a lesser fine, cutting her eyes before jumping off the Special.

By 2:46 Mays had reeled in its share of ditty-bops and B-boys as they disbanded into cliques, disappearing into Mays and other stores along the way. The avenue was famous for collecting the strays and kids who had to be both someplace and no place at all. They milled in droves, stargazing at cheap trinkets imported from Taiwan and going "dis would go good wit my outfit." Their wads of dollars pulled unconsciously out of bus pass wallets and gym socks were always welcomed. Welcomed with loud FM, the monotonous beat that made their bodies dance involuntarily and their eyes glaze for plastic and nylon and 14-carat gold.

All the store owners in the primarily black, brown, and beige strip had accents of some kind or another. Korean or Greek or Island, man. Speak little American. Count change good. Carry baseball bat behind counter. Got big son name Kwan Lee. Walk close behind kids up and down the aisles saying "You want buy?"

Joyce's shoes tapped an almost consistent pattern, keeping up with the rhythms going on in the street. Her neck twisted here and there, as she wondered where were her friends, Cindi and Jay-Jay? They were supposed to hang out and try on clothes at Mays. Actually, Cindi and Jay-Jay would be trying on clothes. Joyce had eighty-five cents, which her mama called pizza money and Joyce called no money. When she finally realized that she would be walking alone her feet dragged, occasionally kicking something in the

3

way. She had wasted too much time with those Davis twins and her friends had left her.

Her eyes were hopelessly caught up on mannequins in flamboyant poses, flaunting winter coats. She grabbed the insides of her jacket pocket to get some warmth from the frayed lining, but the lining couldn't take no more. Why couldn't Joyce be dainty like Cindi and Jay-Jay?

Joyce studied the bony mannequin, its unreal figure like prima ballerina Merryl's. That was what a ballet dancer should look like. Slender, devoid of hips and breasts. At least, that was what Ms. Sobol had in mind for *Sleeping Beauty*.

How do you like that? Ms. Sobol just plain old nixed me from the ballet showcase saying my butt's too big. "It wouldn't look right on stage," she said. "Not with the other girls," she said. "Dancers should never have too much of anything," she said. "It's distracting," she said. "It's not aesthetically pleasing to the audience," she said.

Like my body's a freak machine. Never mind the fact that I have a regular six o'clock extension. No. Never mind the fact that I have an arch. A real arch. Hmmp. And turnout? One-hundred-eighty–degree action. I can do anything a ballerina can do. So she cleans it up by saying my butt is too big for ballet. What does that dry old heifer know about dance anyway? She get me sick. If God gave her a tail it would be all right. We'd all have to have one.

"Well, honey," Joyce informed the mannequin with both hands on hips, "I'm sorry. But God made me a real woman."

It was true. From the neck on down Joyce was a woman. Her fifteen-year-old self had outgrown the brown vinyl jacket along with half the clothes in her closet. If her face wasn't hidden by a mop of natural hair, a sophomore's face full of brightness, smartness, and stupidity would shine through.

She kept walking.

It was just as well that Cindi and Jay-Jay had left her. They'd only want to rehash how Ms. Sobol had begged them to be in the show. Besides, Cindi and Jay-Jay couldn't make Joyce feel better. Not like Sam, who listened to every word, felt every heartbeat, and bought her a cheeseburger. And it *was* Thursday. She didn't have time for Cindi and Jay-Jay anyway.

She would call Sam. He could leave the real estate office and be on the avenue in ten minutes. Sam had money. His wife wouldn't miss the ten dollars that he spent on Joyce. They would go somewhere to eat. Somewhere far from the avenue crowd. And when she came home with extra money she had the story all worked out for her moms. Of course, Minnie Collins was pleased that her daughter was doing something with her time and had no complaints with the After-School Self-Help Program.

Joyce went through a frantic search for Sam's business card. Lord, she had too many papers in her dance bag. Some of them would have to go. Maybe just keep the ones with 90 or better. But that was all of her papers. She liked those big red 92s and 95s, especially from Mr. Weiner, who didn't really want to give them. So she kept them all.

There it was. Buenhogar Realty. She took out her pizza money and called from a nearby booth. Even though he said he'd be there in five minutes, she caught the irritation in his voice. He might not give her ten dollars this time. She might have to let him touch her. That was cool. She could handle it.

The thirty-eight-year-old real estate agent instructed

5

her to be at the corner in front of Woolworth's and to look for a green station wagon. Sometimes he drove a gray Cutlass. He told her that they only had thirty minutes, so she would have to eat fast.

This had been going on for the past two Thursdays. Ha ha. Later for the girls jingling gold bracelets from their boyfriends' nickel-and-dime newspaper routes. Sam was good for a leather coat with fur around the collar.

She remembered how it all began. He would see her passing by the real estate office every day on her way from school. At first she thought he was looking at Cindi and Jay-Jay. But he wasn't. He was looking at her!

It was through her blushing face and eager smile that he learned her age. He studied the situation, smiling harmlessly as she approached. Just as she'd pass, he'd drop his jaw in total disbelief, his eyes lapping up the rhythmic shifts of her behind. If she were seventeen there'd be no problem. But her face looked too young, he contemplated. Then he, a father of four children all older than she, learned her schedule and stood on the corner like a tenth grader waiting for the finest girl in the school to pass by.

But she wasn't the finest girl in the school. She knew that. Joyce was one of those girls that you would have to stare at really hard and say, "if she'd only do this or that she'd truly be a fine, fine babe." But her Levi straights with the seams sewn down the leg, her canary yellow sweatshirt with SOUTHSIDE CREW lettered on it, her high-top black sneakers, and, yes, her mostly uneven, no-logic curly curls often took her out of the running. She didn't even try.

It was all that, plus hiding from mirrors and constantly looking down, that never gave her the slightest clue that something was truly there. So, when Sam said "Hey there, pretty one," she gladly responded.

When she was with her girls he'd only smile at her, keeping their secret. She'd return his smile faintly.

One Thursday he slowed his car down and asked her if she needed a ride home. On the way he bought her two hamburgers and gave her ten dollars. Sam told Joyce that he enjoyed talking to her and would like to continue their talks on Thursdays. Those were the only afternoons he had free. Joyce agreed anxiously.

At each meeting she had something new to tell him, and he seemed to take a genuine interest in the goings-on at school. Sam was good for that. Still, he did make her feel uneasy. He used his hands a lot when he talked, always slapping her knee, shoulder, or, sometimes, thigh. When she'd tense up, he would take his hand back apologetically, explaining that it was normal to use nonverbal communication. He said that in the Cuban culture people touched as a sign of warmth and expression.

Knowing better didn't count for much. Right now, Sam was the best friend she had ever had. Someone to talk to.

"Young lady, I have something I want you to read."

A tall, heavily bearded Muslim dressed in a long white tunic and white balloon pants was looking down at her. Joyce moved along swiftly like the other avenue strays, deaf to the message.

❧ Two

Did he think he was driving a yellow cab? From out
of nowhere his green station wagon, annoyed with its
place at the back of the line, dodged its way in between
the cars that were ahead of it waiting at the red light.
He managed to set off a string of aggravation blaring
down the avenue. It made no difference to him. Their
honking and cussing rolled off him with no effect. He
stuck his arm out the window to flag down the school-
girl standing on the corner by Woolworth's, giving his
horn a steady blow.

No sooner had she jumped in the car and collected
herself, than the station wagon pulled off through a red
light.

In her vision the crowd was reduced to a mass of colorful dots, and the Muslim became a white speck
against the avenue.

"You came just in time." Joyce's lips spread for what
had to be her first smile of the day. "That Muslim dude
was trying to sell me something."

"You hungry?" He disregarded her enthusiasm to attend to his watch. Only a goddamn half hour.

Joyce nodded. She was always hungry. Not that her moms didn't feed her well. She just liked the idea of being taken out. Like a date.

He ordered the hamburgers from the car and drove off. Usually they went inside, sat down, and ate. Sam said they didn't have time for all that today. He had to show a house to some clients at three-thirty. Clients. Welfare cases and college kids looking for housing. No money in that crap.

Joyce made herself immune to Sam's disgust. She noticed Sheilah standing across the street. Sheilah could squash the rumor that Joyce was "always mated, never dated" by seeing her on a date with Sam. Not that Sheilah didn't have her own problems. Sheilah and Joyce came from the same home ground, had gone to JHS One-Nine-Deuce, and talked Southside. And Sheilah dressed Southside boys' style. All that, plus trying out for the boys' varsity basketball team and making the JV squad, made her a social misfit like Joyce.

"Yo, yo, Sheeeeilah! Sheeeeilaaah!"

Joyce succeeded in getting the girl's attention. Six-foot Sheilah peered down to get a better look and yelled back *"Yo, yo, Joycie-o!"*

"You stupid ass! *¿Estás loca?* Stick your head in this window!" Sam ordered, his sallow complexion a shade of green. "Are you simple?" he snapped, keeping his eyes on the road, not wanting to look at her. He came that close to popping her.

Joyce didn't care about the harsh words. What was important was that someone from school had seen her with a guy. Someone knew she had a boyfriend. She waved to the girl who was now a considerable distance away.

"You want the world to know I'm messing around with some kid? My little girl goes to your school. How

9

do you know she ain't friends with my little girl?" He lashed out at her with venom in his Cuban accent. He went on about how stupid she was, in English and Spanish, all the while accelerating down the tricky back road.

The words "my little girl" struck her with the sharpness of profanity.

He refused to name his daughter, as though his regard for the two girls would never relate in any way. Wasn't Joyce his sweet little girl too? Didn't he want to protect her? Cradle her? Love her and give her things like he gave his daughter?

Joyce had figured out who the girl was anyway. With only three Rosarios in the school, one being a boy, the other a stone Rican, it was safe to conclude that Yolanda was Sam's prized daughter. Yolanda, in Joyce's estimation, had a nice wardrobe, a boyfriend named Tito or Rafael, and hung with all the right crowd. She probably snickered at Joyce passing by in the hallways and was in on all of the "There goes Big Butt, the Easy A" jokes.

"Eat your burgers before they get cold." Sam had calmed down considerably. He had to be back in twenty minutes. He parked on a side street.

Joyce ate.

"So what happened at school?"

When it came back to her it all seemed a little silly. She almost didn't want to confide in him, but her need for his understanding overshadowed her insecurities. After all, that was the reason she'd called him. For some understanding. Sam always listened to her problems. He made her feel comfortable spilling out her private thoughts without the fear of being laughed at or reminded that life had bigger problems than hers. There was no way she could talk to her mama—even though Mama said "you can tell me anything." Mama had already been a woman at fifteen, had her own baby, dealt with men—not boyfriends—but men. And Mama had been a ballerina, Miss Ballet Perfect, touring around the world on a real stage with a real dance troupe and with white fluffy skirts. Besides, Mama was too tired to talk after a day of wrestling down sick folks at Jamaica Hospital. Even though Moms never came out and said it, all of Joyce's secrets would be foolishness in Mama's eyes.

"I wanted to try out for the dance showcase at school and my teacher—this old white witch—told me not to even bother."

"They'll have other tryouts," Sam consoled, his voice sweetening at the prospect of opportunity as he concentrated on the seams sewn down the thighs of her dungarees. "Besides," he perked up, snapping himself out of his fantasy, "a girl like you don't want to be in no ballet. That mess puts me to sleep. You wait. In a year or two you could be a dancing girl at Big Joe's Paradise Lounge."

She smiled, pleased that someone knew that she could dance. She'd show that Mizz Sobol.

"Why," he said, "when I first seen you I knew you was a dancer just by the way you walked."

Joyce was embarrassed that Sam had noticed the way her feet turned out when she walked. To him, she must have looked like a black penguin with sneakers.

But Sam's eyes never saw Joyce's feet.

"Girl, I bet you can do some remarkable things with your body."

She nodded proudly. She could do splits, touch the back of her head with her foot, and wrap her legs behind her neck.

"My teacher don't think I have a good body for dance.

She just came right out and said my butt was too big for ballet. I mean, gee. It's bad enough the kids be calling me all kinds of Big Butt, but the teacher? It was embarrassing." Joyce laughed faintly. "At first I was debating whether to go up and put my name on the sign-up sheet. They're doing *Sleeping Beauty*. I didn't want to be the princess or anything like that. I just wanted to be in it. Wear one of them fluffy white skirts. Then when I started to go up there, she says just as loud as day that my butt is too big for ballet and I could just forget this production. I hate that witch. She really can't dance no way. She's just afraid that I'll be too good and show up her girls."

"You're not that big, just average," he informed her, hoping to elicit a challenge. "But I can't really tell by just talking. I still have fifteen minutes," he sang calmly although his patience was wearing thin. He slid over to her side of the vinyl seat. The girl froze, causing Sam to ease up momentarily.

He apologized, putting his arm around her shoulders, stroking her in a fatherly way. When he felt her relaxing, trusting her good friend Sam, he got her to lean her head on his shoulder. His hands were more heavy than a bit. The first ounce of fear whipped through her. She felt a hand sliding down her side and nearing her thighs, which automatically welded together. No one had ever touched her there, so her startled body released a series of warm currents. Regardless, her legs remained locked by the strong muscles developed by hours of practicing pliés.

Sweat beads formed on his neck and forehead, and his breath poured down on her. His free hand didn't care about the costs of getting to her cotton bra underneath the sweater and jacket. It was hopeless; the tattered jacket lining ripped under the demands of his eagerness.

What was she supposed to do? She didn't know how to fight it or if she should. Too much was happening and she didn't know what to do. Curiosity, fear of Mama, and temptation converged. Something like sneaking sips of gin from Mama's cup. If the first sip burns your throat and the second sip makes you silly, then what about the third sip? All the while, her silent voice repeated over and over, "Slow down. You're in over your head." She wanted to listen to her conscience, but the curiosity kept biting. She had to know what was at the other end of those strange feelings. Those sensations that only more touching would alleviate. So she turned off her thinking and slowly released the lock on her legs.

For Sam, that was consent enough.

Joyce heard his zipper ripping and felt heavy hands on her belt buckle. "This won't hurt a bit. You did this before. I know," he told her rather than asked.

But she hadn't. Not even close. The girl they called the Easy A had not even held a boy's hand. Not even a slow dance. She could get pregnant. He was ugly. He was fat. He was old. Even older than Mizz Sobol. He was somebody's daddy. He wasn't Andre Miller, the boy she had planned her first time for.

The sensations that were once racing inside had all of a sudden gone soggy. A jack-in-the-box pounced up and down on her stomach shrieking a hideous laugh, and she found herself scared sober. All she knew was that her moms would kill her if she found out. And all she could see was Moms swinging a rolled-up newspaper and Aunt Em behind her casting out the devil.

She pulled away, pressing against the car door.

"Take me home."

"What?"

"You heard me. Now take me the hell home or else." Her threat was clearly a bluff.

13

He zipped up his pants and backed off immediately. Supposing she caused a scene? How would it look to his wife and his children? Who would they side with? He steamed in silence.

They parked a few blocks down from her house. She could see her home girls, Terri, Gayle, and Lynda sitting on the stoop. Joyce focused straight ahead. His silence put the fear of God in her, although she sat there like the Queen of Sheba daring him to get loud.

"My money."

Her nerve made him stare at her. She refused to blink.

He tore a ten dollar bill from his wallet, crumpled it, and threw it in her lap.

"I try to be nice to you," the words steamed out through the cracks between his teeth, "give you money, something to eat, drive you home, and you keep playing these games." Anger made his voice steady. "Next time, don't bother me if this is what you have in mind. You ain't no damn princess. Probably giving it up to some basketball dude for nothing."

She took the money, grabbed her dance bag, and slammed the car door. She had to make it look good for her girls, who, all a year younger than she, looked up to her, and were watching. "So, fool, next time you'll know better!" She laughed all loud. Joyce shook inside as she walked by the three girls, giving them cool salutations.

Where was she going to get her next ten dollars? Why didn't she let him pop her? It wouldn't have been that bad. Lots of girls fourteen and fifteen were already women. They said it was nothing. It would have been over with so quick she wouldn't have felt it. All she would have had to do was close her eyes and pretend that it was Andre Miller. Tall, golden, green-eyed, curly-headed Andre Miller. And Sam would never have known she was pretending he was Andre Miller.

But she'd feel those heavy hands tearing away at her clothes and his pasty sweat all over her young brown skin. Her eyes would open and there would be potbellied, polyester-pants Sam, old enough to be her daddy.

"Brilliant, Joyce," she said, walking up the stairs of the two-family house, "there go my ten dollars."

❧ Three

Maybe she should tell Mama. Yeah. Right. Sure. Like Mama in her white uniform would understand. And even if she did understand, Mama was never there.

Even as a little girl, Joyce could not remember Mama being there all the time. Her first images of Mama, whom everyone called Minnie, all came from Aunt Em. Mama's big sister, Em, cared for Joyce from the time she was two until she turned ten, while Minnie toured the country with assorted dance ensembles and road companies.

"Lord," Em would say to Minnie on her kinder days, "that's what you get for having Joyce so young. The child's bigger than you."

It was true. Minnie was a tiny thing with some butt and no bust. At twelve, Joycie was an inch taller than Minnie, never went without a bra, and when she walked, the earth knew every step. Joyce was born three weeks before Minnie's sixteenth birthday, a fact that Aunt Em would not let Joyce forget.

"Minnie had to have everything that was going around," Em would say with Joyce's head pressed between her knees as she straightened Joyce's hair Sunday after Sunday. "If it wasn't dancing lessons it was piano lessons, and skates and dresses and the finest boys on the block. And she got tired of everything. Skates ain't been touched, ain't had time for lessons of any kind, and boys? They all seem to get tired after she done give them everything from here to Philly." The hot comb would be resting up near Joyce's ear but the child remained still. The trance was her way of escaping. The less she moved, the sooner she got it over with. The less she said, the less she'd have to hear about her mother. Besides, Joyce got tired of Aunt Em saying those same things about Mama over and over. She knew every "Jesus save her" and "poor fool" by heart. The child grew up thinking her mother's name was Poor Fool.

Sometimes Joyce wondered why Aunt Em in all of her thirty-six years ain't seen no man, no baby, no nothing. As much as she wanted to ask, she never dared, knowing what it could only lead to. Aunt Em was more righteous than a little bit. She was saving her soul for Him, searching for the glory that He had meant for her. Ask her that? "I am a child of God-ah! I am His holy child, praise Him! I cannot sin!" she'd declare, waving the righteous hand in Joyce's face as if cheered on by trumpets. Then the fury in her shrill soprano would subside as she would add, "I was put here to lead you, my child, from the past and present sins of your mama."

And before you knew it, Em would start up on how Minnie got tired of everything she had, including Joyce. Then she would say how her own divine mission was to shepherd the soiled lamb to a bright salvation. Then she'd make the girl kneel and pray. Pray for her soul, pray for her mother's tainted soul and passions— the poor fool, flaunting her flesh under the guise of the stage.

17

But then, everyone was a sinner to Em. Everyone except Pastor Logan, who had to be God Himself taken shape of mortal man in three-piece suits and studded cuffs. Aunt Em gave the church thirty-eight dollars out of each pay so Pastor Logan could go to Egypt, drive a powder blue hog, and give banquets for visiting folk. But did Pastor Logan know Sister Emelia Collins from a speck of black with rooster feathers sticking out of a straw hat? And didn't Em dawn her seldom-seen smiles, inviting the good bachelor over to Sunday dinner every week after services? Of course he never showed.

Strangely enough, he knew Joyce Collins, sitting in a nonchalant daze in the youth choir, while the *amen*s and *well*s passed around. He, with his divine eye, was able to pick out the woman in the ten-year-old child whom Sister Emelia harnessed in girdles and sweeping skirts. He would catch her bopping her pretty head, keeping up with the organ. Why, he even attempted to use the righteous hand of God-ah to save the child from all sin.

Save her from Mama is what they all meant. Trying to get her to come up before the congregation and testify against Mama.

It was much too late for that. Minnie had long infected Joyce with an urgent need to emulate her every pattern. Minnie was just as petite and tough as God would allow. As far as Joyce could see, there wasn't a vulnerable bone in her mother's five-foot body or a weak drop of blood in her veins. If Minnie had some difference with Em, she'd say it to her face, and would laugh and make fun of her sister's *praise Him, hallelujah*s. Joyce would be right behind her mother, so Em wouldn't catch her stuffing her hand in her mouth to keep from hollering.

Minnie and Joycie were like sisters. They were close enough in age. Minnie would do her daughter's hair in bangs, make twists to the side, or pick out a wild "fro." They often went to the avenue to try on clothes and buy meat patties and pizzas at every other stand.

Em didn't believe in that. Em sewed everything Joyce wore, making sure they were all dresses. And Em especially didn't have money to be throwing away on pizza. She had to put that money in church.

Minnie showed Joyce every dance, including combinations from rehearsals, and she knew all the songs on the radio. With nothing better to do, they could make some noise on a Saturday night!

They would be just a-howling, hitting all kinds of notes, mostly swooning and screeching. Salt and pepper shakers served as microphones. When they couldn't handle the high notes, they'd close their eyes and tell Smokey they were with him in spirit. Just about then, Minnie would ask Joyce if she had a boyfriend and if he had green eyes.

"It ain't love unless he got green eyes." Minnie's long reflecting sigh told on her.

"What if he don't have green eyes?"

"Then you'll have strange-looking kids."

"How you know that?"

" 'Cause," Minnie would reply gravely, "your daddy ain't had green eyes and look at what happened to you!"

And they would be just a-howling. Making the devil's noise.

To combat them, Em would begin in all her second soprano force, "Going Up Yonder."

"Well, go soon so we can hear our record!" Minnie would yell up the stairs good and loud.

"Mama," Joyce would almost whisper as though

Aunt Em could hear her breathing, "why Aunt Em act so strange?"

"Emmy not strange."

"Sure."

"All right. A little strange," Minnie conceded.

"Well, then. Why she a little strange?"

"I'll tell you when you get more grown. You too young to understand."

When Sunday mornings came, Minnie and Joyce would still be downstairs, pillows and blankets scattered all on Aunt Em's good carpet. The morning talk show would be coming from the radio, which had been left on all night. Minnie would be half asleep, hearing Em's timid patter coming down the stairs. Em would be clutching one of Joyce's Sunday dresses as if it were alive, getting it ready for a good pressing. Minnie would wake up just long enough to look at her sister as though she were crazy and say, "She's staying with me today." And Minnie would roll over and commence to snore.

The devil.

Sister Emelia Collins went to sit up in the front row at the White Rock Holy and Sanctified House of Prayer alone on those Sundays.

God must have been listening to Joycie, 'cause one Sunday while Em was in church a-praying, Mama said, "Joycie, get all your things together. You're coming to live with me for good. You're gettin' four stepbrothers and stepsisters and a stepdaddy."

But it didn't work out. Mama was always studying nursing or working her part-time job. Mama was never home when Joyce needed her. No more staying up together, talking and laughing. Instead, Joyce had four stepbrothers and stepsisters, which meant changing diapers, braiding heads, and making peanut butter sandwiches. You'd think they were her own doggone kids. And Joyce hated the so-called stepdaddy. He was always looking at her and always yelling about how Minnie was no better than his other women and how she was never home where she belonged.

Gone. That's where Joyce wanted to be. The stepdaddy looked at her every chance he got. So Joyce started sleeping with a steak knife under her pillow and the dresser up against the door. She wouldn't take a bath if he was in the house. She even told Minnie about it. Begged Minnie to take her to work at the hospital. She said she hated him. Something was wrong with that man. Without a thought, Minnie's little hand sent Joyce flying across the room.

See if I ever tell you anything, Joyce silently pledged in steamy puffs, rubbing her stunned face. And that was when the inevitable love war began to fly its colors between the two who were like sisters.

That Friday Minnie stayed home. She sat in the kitchen where she could get the picture. She had the red beans going on the stove. She saw her husband's eyes follow the twelve-year-old girl in and out of the living room. She heard him ordering every five minutes, "Joyce, get me some water, some beer, a sandwich, some this, some that." And each time the girl came in the room his eyes dogged her every movement.

"So you like that dancin' they teachin' up at the school?" He caught Joyce by the arm before she could make a getaway after bringing him his beer.

"Yep," she replied, not looking at him.

"So, uh, what kind of dancing you do, girl? How come I ain't never got no show?"

Joyce didn't speak.

"Come on, girl," he motioned to her. "Let's see some of this dancing."

Well God bless a mama. Minnie had heard enough and flew out into the living room with the pot of burning beans in her hand. He settled back in the chair all childlike, as if he couldn't figure out what was going on.

"Joyce, get your things."

The girl ascended the stairs in a mad flight of ecstasy. They were leaving! She began throwing her things in a shopping bag angrily.

The kids were all around asking what she was doing, where she was going, and if they could go too. She drew on all of her maturity, and stated, "I'm leaving."

Joyce was so happy that she couldn't hear the screaming and cussing going on downstairs. She picked up her bag. Just as she got to the stairs she heard a thud. She saw her mother on the floor rubbing her side, red beans all over the place. A wildness flooded her and she jumped on top of the man who put his hands on her mama, bringing him down to the ground. She kept on beating him in the chest and in the face. The kids came running around screaming, "Don't you hit my daddy!" But Joyce and Minnie never once let up on the pitiful lump of a man practically dragged out of his clothes.

It took them no time to throw their things together and run down the block before he got his strength up to come after them. They laughed all the way down the street. Neither knew where they were going, but didn't it feel good to be like sisters, running together!

She sat up in the window with her knees up against the radiator. She felt a tremendous ache to tell Mama things. Just things. But Mama wasn't there. Not like sisters. Not no more.

❧ Four

The next morning Joyce couldn't get up fast enough. Had to tell Cindi and Jay-Jay all about how she dealt with Sam. And they'd be impressed like Lynda, Terri, and Gayle were. But first came the obstacle. Passing by Buenhogar Realty.

An involuntary warmth flooded her as she approached the real estate office. She walked slowly by the office looking for a way out of the thick mud that their brief encounter had left her in. The green station wagon hadn't pulled into its spot yet. Joyce aimed her middle finger at an empty front desk.

She made a dash to catch the bus pulling away from the stop, her dance bag banging carelessly into her side. Joyce had to kick down the door before the bus driver gave in, disgusted with himself for not leaving her. She dropped her money down the slot, waiting for the driver to acknowledge her.

"You didn't have to slam the door in my face."

"I didn't have to let you in, either," he retorted, ready for her. They had this conversation regularly during the school week, so he didn't bother to look up at her. She was nobody.

23

Embarrassing, she thought, then pushed her way through the standing crowd to be near Cindi and Jay-Jay.

Joyce looked at Cindi and Jay-Jay and hungered for their popularity. She had to be part of their crew. Once she was associated with them, life at Cardozo would be fat cake. Cindi, Joyce, and Jay-Jay. It even sounded like a together crew. And she knew she could win them as true friends.

Except when they were with their boyfriends, Cindi and Jay-Jay were always together. All gossip at Cardozo began with their names in hopes of destroying their relationship. The loyalty between Cardozo's finest juniors was a careful one, allowing no room for falling-outs or misunderstandings. As far as close friends went, they had each other. They dressed similarly, planned their absences for the same days, took the same classes, and achieved more or less the same grades.

In a vote, Cindi would be the favorite among the two to despise. She made no bones about whom she didn't like, rarely made a friendly gesture, and was more conceited than a touch. Jay-Jay was her only female friend. Rather than going through the trouble of speaking, Cindi made expressions with skillfully arched eyebrows and pinched nose, ranging from *oh really?* to a dubious *hmmp.* Only the thick West Indian clues in her voice and the waves at the root of her brown-near-blonde tresses saved her from being Caucasian.

Jay-Jay was thought of as the friendly one. Born in the States, her Island blood surfaced and submerged at given moments. When Jay-Jay was with her West Indian friends she was that, when she was with her stateside friends she became that—she couldn't help it. She was a fiend for conversation. Gossiping was her means for measuring her own nearness to perfection. However, unlike her counterpart, her own beauty was not enough. Despite her shoulder-length hair and her fine features, she had an insatiable need for compliments. And being with Cindi was, in her mind, the ultimate compliment.

As tight as Cindi and Jay-Jay were, you couldn't tell Joyce that they'd never let her in. All the while that Joyce had pursued them, Cindi and Jay-Jay igged her. That is until Joyce showed up for Dance II doing six o'clock extensions the way people breathed. Cindi and Jay-Jay had no other choice but to befriend her. Jay-Jay wasted no time before drilling her for her background. What studio did she belong to? What techniques did she study? What shows did she work in?

Joyce's first week of classes told all. After watching her at the barre and going across the floor, they could relax. She was either a gymnast or her stretch and turnout were mere physical accidents, whereas they were classically trained. Joyce was just pushed into Dance II by the folk dance instructor who supposedly saw classical talent in her and thought she could benefit from the visiting professional.

Unfortunately, there was no shaking the girl. After Cindi and Jay-Jay offered the slightest bit of interest, Joyce hung on to them for dear life.

"Yo, ladies, what's up?" Joyce greeted them with her usual enthusiasm, which they termed loudness.

"Nothing really," Jay-Jay said.

"Well I just broke up with my old man. I had to nix that in a hurry," Joyce told them coolly.

News to them. They glanced at each other suspiciously through corners of their eyes. Big Butt was the girl that everyone said they had. But be seen with her? Actually go with her?

"Yeah," Joyce confirmed with an eagerness to divulge details. "He was too old to really hang out. I had to cut him loose."

"Well how old was he?" Jay-Jay inquired. Even if it was over it was still worth the scoop. "A senior?"

"The big three-eight," Joyce replied, waiting for their approval.

"Thirty-eight? My father's thirty-nine." Jay-Jay was thoroughly impressed.

"Hmmp." Cindi doubted the story immediately. Her quick glance at Jay-Jay suggested that they should pursue it.

"Well," Jay-Jay said, picking up her cue, "a man like that don't want a high school hang-out partner."

"He wants a woman," the other interjected.

"So, were you woman enough or just a big baby?"

"It wasn't *even* like that." Joyce defended her story loud enough to be heard by everyone on the Special. "I could deal."

"Grown men are harder to please, you know," Jay-Jay began, all the while nudging Cindi. *Can you believe this? Isn't she just too stupid?*

You know how it is, the other smiled back.

Easy A+ with Big Butt.

Jay-Jay went on. "Grown men don't respond to just anything. That's why I can't be bothered with a dude over twenty-five, honey." She borrowed an Atlanta drawl to add to her credibility. Twenty-five-year-old man? Her good and proper Southern daddy would kill her if she even thought about it!

"Maybe you didn't give him enough variety," Cindi said, managing a whole sentence.

Joyce rolled her eyes to indicate boredom. "He got everything he could handle."

The subject was closed. Cindi and Jay-Jay would talk

during first period. But there was no shaking Joyce. And who wanted to be associated with a girl with her rep?

Cindi and Jay-Jay whispered at every opportunity. They could barely get rid of her while they changed for Dance II and hurried to the studio. They nodded to Merryl, who led the class in barre, and took their respective places behind her. There was no time to chat. Joyce located them and forced another girl to move so she could be near them.

Joyce's uniform stood out among the whites, pinks, baby blues, and blacks. She took class barefoot, wore navy blue stirrup tights and a mandarin orange leotard with an elastic belt around the waist that dramatized her proportions, making her waist a narrow stem for her heart-shaped buttocks. Her legs had a nice way about them and looked good in stockings on those rare occasions that she wore a dress. Her breasts were ample but not her main feature. Standing in profile at the barre, Joyce ruined the line of twenty would-be Makarovas, all slight in stature, with her blue tights and her big butt.

Ann Sobol, née Anya Sobolevsky, made her entrance wearing pink hand-knitted warm-ups, rolled at the waist to expose her Joffrey T-shirt. Her face was always tremendously made up, with two or three shades of pink and purple fighting to bring out her already huge eyes. If it weren't for the bulge in her stomach she would be a perfect stick figure.

Joyce didn't approve of what ballet did for the body, and Ms. Sobol was living proof of that. Being able to see the woman's bones made it no better. Her feet were protected by a thin sheath of skin, and a huge muscle on top of her ankle swelled up when she folded—not pointed, but folded—her foot in half. Joyce could never

27

understand why Cindi and Jay-Jay would remark with admiration and awe, "Look! Look! Sobol's feet are superior." As far as Joyce could see, that woman had absolutely nothing on her body to make a man look twice. At best she was maybe twenty-eight, which was as good as near death to Joyce.

Why couldn't a regular gym teacher teach Dance II? The regular gym teachers didn't single you out " 'cause your butt is big."

The dance instructor was forever tagging her students by whatever words were handy, mainly those referring to their attributes. Never their names. Sheilah was "that tall one" and another girl was simply "you, with the thighs." Joyce was forever "blue tights, big butt." The ballerina at the far right of the barre was Ann Sobol's most adored "Mademoiselle" Merryl.

Sobol cleared her throat to get the class' attention. "Rehearsal at four for the fairies and at six for my principal," she acknowledged Merryl on an endearing note. She nodded to the pianist in the corner, who responded with two flat notes. The class tendued to second.

"Two demi, two grande, in third, closed fourth," she stated, glancing around the studio, "and finish in fifth. I want to see line. Clear line. Up and down. Line. And one, two . . ."

During the class' opening positions Ann Sobol went through the roll book. Once the brown book was tucked underneath her arm, she began pacing watchfully along the barre, issuing corrections and rare praises. Of course, Mademoiselle Merryl could do no wrong. Cindi and Jay-Jay earned their usual nods of approval, eating up the little compliments as though they were bread. She never bothered with Sheilah who was better suited for basketball. Instead, her guidance was saved for one student who never realized the privilege of being in the teacher's eye. The student with the most potential and the least discipline. The one who wore blue tights.

"Tuck that butt under!" the woman insisted, gravely offended by the sight of the student's posture. "Come on," she said, pushing down on Joyce's buttocks with the palms of her hands. Joyce wanted to turn around and slap her. She managed to hold her arm in second position, her fingers filled with tension, almost fisting. Cindi and Jay-Jay were whispering, all the while suppressing their laughter.

"No! No! Don't let your pelvis fall! Lift up! Watch your butt! Look at what you're doing!" Ms. Sobol screamed. "Now lift up in here," she instructed while holding her student's rib cage in place, "and tuck under. Right! That's it." She finally abandoned Joyce to harass another student with a less severe problem.

What's wrong with white people, anyway? Don't they know that this is just how black folks are made? How come she don't see nothing wrong with any of these no-tail, no-hips, no-nothing nons? Just me.

The barre was only the beginning. Tendues, dégagés, frappés, all wrong. Of course everyone had to turn around to watch Joyce do it wrong for the tenth time. That is, everyone but Mademoiselle Merryl, too busy looking in the mirror as she balanced in fifth. Merryl was probably unaware that Joyce was in the same class.

Finally the best part of the barre came. Joyce loved grands battements or any kind of leg extension. Hers were noticeably higher than anyone else's, even Merryl's. She plunged into them determined to shine, even if it was for a few minutes.

"It doesn't matter how high the leg goes up." Sobol's

voice became louder as she neared Joyce. "What matters is that the leg is correct."

Joyce felt Sobol's breath upon her neck. She felt a cold hand gripping her leg in midmotion.

"Not from the hip!" Ann Sobol's right hand held Joyce's hip firmly while the other hand wrestled with the elevated leg, trying to jerk it out of its socket. "You have a different turnout. You are too lazy. You have to work it just right."

The truth, Joyce summed up, was that the dance instructor couldn't stand to have her precious Merryl shown up. The truth was that Sobol would never say "Class, look at how well Joyce does it." No. The absolute truth was that Sobol would always say, "Class, will you look at what she's doing wrong."

And one two three, two two three, I hate ballet two three. I hate ballet two three. . . .

❧ Five

The dull bell signifying the end of the first period set off a customary round of applause throughout the studio. While four rows of demure ballerinas bowed in appreciation to Ms. Sobol, then to the pianist who didn't seem to care, Joyce concealed in her delicate croisé fourth position bow, a firm fist.

The locker room became a swarm of orange-and-blue lacrosse uniforms among pastel shades of leotards and tights from Dance II. The gym leaders, distinguished by white uniforms and braided whistle chains, dressed in their own corner, equipped with a couch, full-length mirrors, and bigger lockers.

Joyce didn't believe in undressing after class and always kept her dance gear on under her street clothes. She didn't appreciate anyone, boy or girl, staring at her for a good length of time. The thought of peeling down to her underwear terrified her. She knew they all wanted to stare at her round tail and snap on her underwear. Her white cotton underwear was inferior to the colorful matching sets that the other girls wore. She noticed how they lingered in their colored underwear, talking and laughing and showing off what they had.

Merryl was an extreme case. Merryl never wore panties or a bra under her leotards. Merryl didn't mind people looking at her nude or otherwise. She never seemed to notice them, the queer child.

Joyce fiddled with her combination lock, trying not to appear fascinated by the skillful choreography, the art of dressing as executed by two virtuosos. The powders, lotions, and perfumes were followed by pantyhose, blouses, sweaters, and slacks, ending with the application of eyeshadow, lipstick, blush—stare, stare, and smile. It was in the final steps of the dance that Cindi and Jay-Jay blossomed into full character. They stared at their images unblinking, giving their eyes, lips, and hair the final corrections and approving nods, without the least concern for being gawked at.

Joyce, on the other hand, couldn't be forced to look at herself in the mirror. Even in class, she gazed at the floor to avoid the confrontation between herself and her face. She was terrified of seeing what everyone laughed at.

"There goes Princess Aurora and her royal towel." Joyce directed her sarcasm at Merryl coming out of the shower stall.

"The girl knows her stuff," Cindi defended Merryl.

"She has perfect feet," Jay-Jay added, with a sincerity that was even too much for Jay-Jay. "I'll bet Sobol's gonna let her do her solo en pointe. Everyone else will be en demi. At least the show will look somewhat professional."

Cindi agreed, with arched eyebrows and a slow nod. "Merryl's definitely gonna come off like a pro."

Joyce was disappointed. The two juniors were betraying a bond. They were probably just saying that because Merryl was dressing nearby. Merryl couldn't really dance.

"And we're really lucky to have Sobol this term. It's not often that we get visiting professionals," Cindi said.

"That's right. Take advantage of everything she has to offer."

"That is if you're going to be professional," Cindi said. "Not everyone can be professional."

"Yeah, not like us," Joyce included herself.

"But check it out." Cindi beamed while waving an imaginary wand. "I just knew she wanted me to be the Lilac Fairy. No one else—except you, Jay-Jay—has the technique. I can see my costume now. I just *adore* chiffon."

"So Joyce, why didn't you try out?" Jay-Jay inquired.

"Are you ready for this?" Joyce smiled, letting them in on the secret. "Sobol said my butt was too big for ballet and I could just forget it." She then paused, turning sharply to catch anyone who might be listening. "You know what it was?"

They leaned closer.

"She wouldn't know what to do if there was more than two of *us* in it. She couldn't really deal with that."

"But if you're good it don't matter," Cindi told her. Of course she could say that. Dance Theatre of Harlem, Ailey's, and Graham. She had it like that.

"You know, my sister had the exact same problem," Jay-Jay offered sympathetically. Cindi eyed her suspiciously. "'Cept she had a big chest. When the girl moved, *everything* moved! I mean, the girl had some monster jugs!" They all fell out laughing. Cindi and Jay-Jay especially, because Jay-Jay was an only child.

"My poor sister couldn't get no play. Ballet? The girl could tour jeté her life away. But when it came to costumes with spaghetti straps and plunging necklines she could just hang it up."

"So what did she do?" Joyce asked.

"She auditioned for the American Dance Conservatory. All that counts there is how good you are." Cindi and Jay-Jay knew all about the Dance Conservatory, both having been rejected.

"Why don't you think about transferring, especially if you can't change your problem." *That would be a good way to get rid of her,* Jay-Jay thought. After all, the girl took no hints.

"I just might do that," Joyce said.

"I think their transfer auditions are coming up. If you ask Ms. Sobol to hook you up with some choreography, your chances of getting in are even better," Jay-Jay said.

That dried up biddy? Not on a nickel.

"So what if you're not classically trained?" Jay-Jay offered. "You could probably do African dance."

"Probably," Cindi corroborated.

"They have ethnic dance groups all over South Jamaica. You should join one," said Jay-Jay.

"You should," came the echo.

"If I don't make those transfer auditions I might have to look into an ethnic dance group. I'd do anything to dance."

A flat "good luck" came from Cindi and Jay-Jay as they snapped shut their makeup cases. The possibility of improvement just didn't exist. They believed in every ounce of their beauty and couldn't be told otherwise.

"So, are you going to Andre's gig?" Jay-Jay asked.

Joyce said nothing. Andre Miller.

"You don't know about Andre's party?"

Jay-Jay took out her invitation from her square

leather bag, flashing the white index card penned in green Magic Marker before Joyce's eyes. Must have been written by Andre himself.

"I didn't get an invite." Joyce pretended to be unaffected.

"That don't matter. Go with us. I mean, it's only a house party," said Jay-Jay.

Cindi nudged Jay-Jay just short of hitting her. She was going too far.

"Isn't he too fine?" Joyce cooed, indulging in a brief daydream with Andre telling her that it would last forever. Joyce was so far gone that she didn't notice her friends signaling each other, amused by her expression.

Cindi's quick glance stopped Jay-Jay from saying, "Andre? He's OK." If anything, Cindi's look told her, Joyce was good for a few laughs. Jay-Jay used to go with Andre. No big thrill. She needed someone to tell her how fine *she* was looking instead of her being a mirror for some dude.

"Isn't he?" the two girls rejoined simultaneously, waiting for Joyce to complete her thoughts.

"He's so tall," Joyce said, feeling safe.

"So why don't you come to the party with us? We'll introduce you," Cindi went along, her invitation dripping of sweetness.

"As far as I know, he's not talking to anyone," Jay-Jay told her. *Wouldn't it be funny if she went to the party and Andre got her up in his room and she took off all of her clothes and we'd all bust in and laaaaaaugh? Hysterical.*

"I do like him," Joyce confided. "And I know he likes me too. But you know Andre. Got to be cool. Laying for the right moment."

"Right."

"Can't wait 'til Friday. I have to get something new to wear. Thanks for inviting me."

"De nada."

Why shouldn't they include her in their party? They were her friends. They had invited her to Cindi's Sweet Sixteen.

Cindi's Sweet Sixteen could have been Joyce's. Minnie bought Joyce a new dress, made up her face, and did her nails. Cindi and Jay-Jay almost didn't recognize her and couldn't wait to get an opportunity to discuss her new look.

Cindi's Sweet Sixteen was in the city at the Hawaii Kai. All the girls had their eyes on a LaSalle cadet sitting with his parents. The cadet sent the waiter over to the Sweet Sixteen table with a note for Joyce. He wanted to have his picture taken with her, and she was exploding with thrill. After they posed for two pictures he asked in the most polite manner what was her name, where did she attend school, and what sorts of things did she enjoy. He apologized for taking her away from her friends and said "Thank you, Miss Joyce Alicia Collins, for the pleasure of your company." She could see the words coming out of his lips in a delicate cursive script. It was both foreign and wonderful.

Cindi did not approve. "How could you go over there and do that?"

Being with Cindi and Jay-Jay wasn't always a privilege. There were times after football games when Cindi and Cliff, Jay-Jay and Stevie were arm in arm, walking all slow while Joyce just lingered behind them. There were times on the crowded Special that Cindi and Jay-Jay sat on their boyfriends' laps, their heads pressed together while they whispered so low that only their lips could be seen moving. Joyce usually hung over them, just there.

If she could only have the kinds of clothes Cindi and Jay-Jay had, everything would be different. That was precisely why she had to get a job today, be paid by Friday, buy her outfit, and be ready for the party.

After school she stepped inside Mays, equipped with her social security card and working papers. Today she'd tear down the walls that prevented her from being one of the crew. She'd get a job, set up her audition—just for the status of having auditioned—and most important, she would be Andre's woman. Even if she didn't have all new clothes, being Andre's woman would always get her a seat on the Special, invited to all of the functions, and respect from everybody.

She approached the security guard, who appeared more suspect than the shoppers.

"I'm looking for a job."

"You can work for me," he said, scoping her up and down.

"Hey, that's my lady you're talking to." Andre busted down the glass door and killed the guard with a single roundhouse kick. "Baby are you all right? Did he touch you? Daddy's gonna make it all right."

"Just tell me where Personnel is."

"Third floor, baby. Up the escalators and all the way to the back."

Optimism took over. She could make more money as a cashier in Mays than what Sam could give her. All of a sudden the ten dollars that he'd given her each time she'd seen him was mere chump. She was going to be the best-dressed girl at Andre's party. She could step out in a brand-new leather coat and matching boots. Then, like magic, everyone would like her. Things would change.

Things had to change. Cardozo had rules. Social rules. Even the black clique spoke a little different and socialized different from the folks on the home ground. They weren't white, but they weren't 'round-the-way either.

And the boys at school? They had definite rules for the girls that they would be seen with. The right girl was never laughed at, didn't resemble Easy A's mama, and never wore the same thing twice in one week.

It all started during Joyce's first week of school when Marvin and Melvyn decided they both liked her. Since neither could have her, and everyone made jokes about her round tail, they did the next best thing. They bragged as loud as day that they both got over on Joyce. Naturally, every other dude in the tenth grade had to defend his rep by topping the twins' story with an even better one. They justified it by telling themselves that someone was getting it if they weren't, and that any girl who looked like that couldn't possibly be no innocent. Other girls kept their distance so as not to be linked with "that girl Joyce, who must be doing it with Lottie, Dottie, and everybody."

Why couldn't she be like Cindi and Jay-Jay? Social untouchables. They had everything. Money meant nothing to their families. They got their hair done in the city, went to concerts, took summer vacations in Puerto Rico and the Virgin Islands, and had beautiful Sweet Sixteens. They studied Graham at Graham Studios, Horton at Alvin Ailey, pointe at the Dance Theatre of Harlem, and when they couldn't be bothered with the hustle of the city, they were the darlings of Bernice Johnson's Studio on Merrick Boulevard.

Naturally, any boy felt privileged to be seen with them. They were so fine and petite that you'd never hear any dirty jokes with their names or bodies involved. Men never dogged them in the streets or tried to get a fast feel in a crowd.

38

To be Cindi and Jay-Jay was the life.

"Can I help you?"

"Yes. I'd like an application for a job," she managed in her clearest voice.

He wanted to say no but changed his mind and tore off a sheet from the thinning application pad.

"Do you have working papers?"

She nodded, searching through her wallet.

"Okay," he said, gesturing for her to put the wallet away. "Take your time and fill it out over there."

She made herself deaf to the hopelessness in his voice and blind to the other fifty people filling out applications for the same job.

Money, money! Joyce whipped out the door, leaving the security guard and mannequins behind. Her first week's pay was already spent as she sailed past windows. She saw leather coats, boots, new leotards, a dance bag. They'd probably call her house the moment she stepped in the door. She had to get home fast.

She put a hot bounce in her step, ignoring the eyes that she attracted and the kisses she inspired from men and boys alike. She was a rhythm maker with a hot scat, dodging the Muslim with his donation cup and his incense. From across the street she saw the long lines formed at the Youth Employment Center. She banked the corner like a runaway plane.

Without warning her brisk strides were cut to a halt. Her confidence came undone. There was no way that she could turn around or down another street or duck into a store. They had already spotted her coming toward them. She couldn't decide whether to look down at the ground or into a store window. Her heart stuttered. Andre too-fine-to-be-forgotten Miller; Andre too-cool-to-be-cold Miller; Andre Miller, the lady thriller.

It was too soon. She had only spoken to Cindi and

Jay-Jay this morning. She needed to get her act together. What was she going to say? Her hair, she thought, glancing at her reflection in a window. Was it too late to pat her hair into shape? *No. Don't do that. He'll just think you're trying to be cute for him.*

What were they saying?

She knew. Jay-Jay was telling him everything that Joyce thought about him. All of her secrets.

The stupid block refused to end. The little hairs on her back and neck stood up. Had she passed them yet? She wasn't even on them.

Andre's teeth were gleaming. Cindi and Jay-Jay were also smiling.

"Hi Cindi, Jay-Jay. Hello Andre."

They nodded.

"So, what's up?"

"Not a damn thing," Andre let her know in sub-zero chill. "Why do you ask?"

She couldn't speak. They stood there waiting for her to crack under the pressure of their eyes.

"Check you later," Joyce said before turning. She heard a storm of laughter just as she entered the bus terminal. She heard "Not that cow!" distinctly from Andre Miller, the lady thriller. "Me? Be seen with that?"

Cindi and Jay-Jay could still be heard, cackling on top of his loud put-down.

Andre not-really-down Miller.

✿ Six

"He does like me. I know it. He was just being cool because they were there. Some friends. They just want him for themselves. Told him all lies about me. That's cool.

"I don't need them anyway. None of them. And if I get this job, look out. I'll be dressing so fine that not even Cindi and Jay-Jay can hang with me. And Andre? I can hear him now: 'Baby, don't be that way. You know you're the star.' And wait. The whole class will beg me to save the show because Merryl's jamming it up left and right.

"Ha. See if I don't laugh right in their faces and tell them exactly where they can—"

"Girl, what are you mumbling about?" Minnie's words brought her back to reality.

Whatever Joyce tried to say was stifled in a flush of embarrassment.

"Talking to yourself?"

The *Times* was spread open in a brown lounge chair with Minnie somewhere behind it, studying the events of the day. Minnie's shift must have changed because there she sat, waiting to inspect Joyce's class notes, homework assignments, and exams. Dinner was cooking too.

"Ma, did you ever audition?"

"Did I ever!" Minnie exclaimed. The joy of dance was still deep within her. She put the paper down and turned to Joyce quizzically with "what on earth?" all over her mouth. "But that was years ago," Minnie brushed it off.

Joyce only became more interested. "For Broadway? What shows?"

"Daughter, I auditioned for every and any little black company and production that popped up. Wasn't many," she said.

"So what did you do? What did you wear?"

"Everything, child!" Minnie said as visions of her young dancing body went spinning by. "Everything. Ballet. Jazz. Dunham. Anything. I went to all the auditions. Mostly cattle calls. My best audition was for Thelma Hawkins. I put together a spiritual and had on this white skirt with ruffles. I tore up one of Emmy's good sheets. Thought she like to kill me!" Reflection colored her face with youthful devilment. "But girl, when I finished with my audition I knew I was in. I put so much feeling in it you could say I moved them with the spirit!"

"Praise Jesus!" they testified, mocking Sister Emelia.

"Now hush. We shouldn't be laughing at Emmy."

"But Ma, she's crazy."

"Loneliness and a whole lot of other things will do that to a woman." Minnie took a moment for solemn remembrances.

"What other things?" Joyce wanted to know.

"I'll tell you when you're grown."

Joyce sucked her teeth. Ma had been saying that for years. Joyce didn't much care. Aunt Em was just a crazy old babe who thought the Holy Spirit was more important than Joyce taking dance lessons and being like her mama.

"Now, what's all this about auditions?" Minnie asked, wrinkling her tweezed brow.

"I want to audition for the American Dance Conservatory," *and show up Cindi and Jay-Jay and Merryl and Ms. Sobol,* she concluded silently.

Minnie said nothing, only making a vague expression that was somewhere between not taking her seriously and being afraid to.

"Say something, Ma."

Minnie released a long sigh, shaking her head. Here we go again, she thought, seeing herself as Joyce, just a few years ago.

"I thought you liked the dance program at your school."

"It's so corny, Ma."

"Is it, now."

"All they want us to do is that dry ballet nonsense. I mean, that's not what's happening."

"What do you expect from the conservatory? Finger poppin' and jumpin' and carrying on? They gonna ballet your butt in triplicate plus a few other things you won't like. So come on with the real story. Why you want to transfer all of a sudden?"

Joyce sucked her teeth once more.

"I told you about doing that," Minnie warned. "Now tell me. What's going on?"

"I hate that school. They all make fun of me because of my behind. The teacher told me to forget about *Sleeping Beauty* 'cause I wouldn't look good with the other skinny little witches on stage."

"She said that?"

"She might as well."

"Well. Are you good enough to be in this show?"

Joyce said nothing.

"Well, girl? Say something. I can't go up to the school fussing and carrying on if you can't dance."

"I can outdance them all. That teacher just don't like me. That's all."

Minnie hummed an *um hmm*.

"I don't care if I never see that school or no one else in it. Especially that Andre. Not after what he did."

"Do? What he do?" Minnie jumped out of her chair. "Am I gonna have to kill some poor mama's son?"

"No, Mama," Joyce said right away. "It ain't even like that."

"Then what?"

"I told Cindi and Jay-Jay that I liked Andre and they was just pretending to be my friend and they told him some lies about me and they was all laughing in my face at the bus terminal."

First came relief. "So now you know those two ain't your friends."

"Yeah. I know."

"But, you know, Joyce, none of these boys will give you the proper time of day if you don't take better care of yourself."

Joyce got offended immediately and stopped herself just short of sucking her teeth.

"You fifteen years old and always in them dern sneakers and that ragamuffin sweatshirt. You's too womanly to be dressing like some wild junior high school ditty-bop. That was fine last year, but you're in high school. A middle-class high school. You should be more ladylike. Do something neat with that hair. Can't even see your face."

"Aw Maaaa."

"At this rate, the only one come knocking on my door

will be some little bum hanging around the Forty Projects instead of some semi-decent nice boy. And I'm a-tell you, girl, the boys in your school aren't like these little hoods in South Jamaica. They ain't bringing little sneaker-boppers home to meet they mama."

Mama was on their side. What did she know about boys staring at her booty all day long? Miss Ballet Perfect.

"I just want to go to the Dance Conservatory."

With a smugness that Joyce resented, Minnie told her casually, "If that's what you want to do, go ahead. But don't think you can get up there and finger pop. The competition will be ready with their technique, so be prepared."

Yeah. Right. Sure. This ain't like your auditions in the Stone Ages way back when they was wearing wooden toe shoes.

"Yes, Ma."

"You have to be clear in your movements and put some feeling in it, and point them toes. They still look for the little things. And girl, hold your head up while you're dancing. Be proud."

Easy for you to say. You don't know.

Sometimes all Minnie could do was look at her daughter and sadly shake her head. In some ways, Joyce was her child like she was no other mother's. And that was the scary part—seeing Joyce's mistakes before she made them, having once been a hard fifteen herself.

Joyce crept around the apartment like an elf on the Saturday of the audition. She was careful not to disturb Minnie on her day of rest. She tiptoed down the stairs in an exaggerated first position with her dance bag slung over her shoulder, tokens in her hand. For a sec-

45

ond she hated her neighborhood and wanted to kick something in her path to let her hatred out as she headed for the subway. She became immersed in the escape as if the air around her was extremely thick and reaching the other side would be cleansing. There was something in the air that made South Jamaicans lethargic. She felt it momentarily and weaved through the stupored crowds who were busy gazing into windows of stores owned by Koreans.

A block ahead she saw a group of what had to be dancers loading equipment onto a van. They wore purple jackets with some long foreign name on it. African words. And there were girls with long braids doing last-minute rehearsals and a tall man directing traffic. And as she passed through the group her eyes touched eyes with a guy carrying congas, and she felt strange because his eyes were looking at her face. Her *face.* And the tall man directing traffic said, "We could use another girl in this piece," but he couldn't have been talking to her, or could he? *No. Couldn't be.* She was already down the block and gone.

She raced past coffee shops, pizza places, and hot dog vendors, consumed with a newfound snobbery. Dancers don't eat before auditions, she told her grumbling stomach.

She couldn't wait to get up there and do her dance. It didn't matter if she wasn't in that *Sleeping Beauty.* It was probably gonna be dry anyway. Not like her dance. Her dance was alive. It would make anyone say, "Now that girl can dance." Then she could break it to Ann Sobol in her most articulate voice, saying, "I'll no longer be attending your raggedy classes. I'm with the American Dance Conservatory." And Cindi and Jay-Jay? "I'll try to make your little *Sleeping Beauty* production, that is if I'm not too busy doing *real* dance." Ha! The looks on their faces!

Joyce paid no attention to the usual comments from men waiting on the sidewalk for some young thing to trot by. She didn't jump back and get evil when they yelled, "Gat damn, baby! Are they real?" or "Good golly, girl, tear the house down!" By the time she was twelve she knew her first name was either Good Golly or Stack Attack. Aunt Em used to make her pray to be a nice girl. Men don't say that to holy and sanctified girls.

Today she silently begged them to leave her alone. She had something to do and she couldn't have anyone bothering her. Her mind had to be a certain way to get through the audition, and she couldn't be dancing with her head down. But no . . .

A blue Ford finally made its bid after tailing her from block to block. She refused to offer the driver a glance. Aw, she was just teasing him, he thought, steadily cranking down his window.

He blew his horn at her.

No, she don't want no ride.

"Yo babe, can I come?"

She said no. *Can't you see I'm a dancer?*

"Say baby, I love the way you move that thang." He reached out to grab her.

She disappeared down the subway and all that he grabbed was her dust.

It was dark and musty in the subway. She moved to the middle of the platform, trying not to stare at the derelict woman: an Arab in sweaters, droopy army socks on flea-bitten legs, sooty Caucasian skin, and a painfully distorted mouth. Her home was the steps of the subway. Leaves of a three-week-old Sunday *Times* were her blanket.

Joyce's attention was diverted to a boy approaching her with rapid speed carrying a home stereo on his shoulder. She summed up that he also lived in the subway. He wore a dingy warm-up suit, more than likely his only clothing, and his hair was intricately corn-rowed underneath a knitted cap pulled up at the top in B-boy style. He darted by her, calling out "loose joints," bruising her nose with his funky body odor. His voice echoed until it was completely overtaken by the rumble of the oncoming E train.

She sat comfortably in her split, unimpressed by the obvious performances enacted by eager dancers waiting to audition. Everywhere she turned there were either superficial reunion scenes or loud chatter about other auditions. She could barely believe these people were her age, with their sophisticated display. They probably flocked to auditions every Saturday morning, belonged to the union, chain-smoked, ate whole wheat bread, did PCP, and read *Back Stage* religiously.

She watched other dancers in corners rehearsing their audition pieces. Their curious gestures weren't dance at all, Joyce decided. She shrugged and gazed at a couple practicing a lift. Ballet, she concluded. Once she heard the twinkle twinkle of their ballet music she dismissed them as competition. White girls. What did you expect?

"Number nine."

The prickly bristles that stood up on her back lay down against her skin when Aretha blessed the studio with winding moans of "Amazing Grace." Although Joyce knew every inch of the record, she hung onto the profound sweetness in the guidance of the diva, who told Joyce when to leap, contract, or turn. Everyone watching her from the panel and from the sidelines faded to a blur. Her only purpose was to absorb the gospel and translate it into depth and motion.

Minnie had told her not to worry about what came next, but to do whatever came naturally. She had the divine flow on her side. Her dance was partially choreographed and mostly Joyce. No one in her ballet class could come close to unearthing the feeling that came to Joyce when she was free to do her own movement.

Her skirt rippled in the excitement of swooping turns and Graham-like prances. She built from one moment onto the next, clearly testifying with Aretha and the piano rolls. When it was time to come down off her dance, she elevated her leg until she appeared to do a standing split, with one arm eternally reaching, seeking.

"Thank you."

They were all staring at her as if she were naked. The next dancer waiting to perform for the panel gestured impatiently for her number to be called.

Joyce sat by her dance bag, watching the other dancers. The ballet dancers for the most part attempted pointe. One couple performed a pas de deux from *Copelia*. And the modern dances! Nothing like her dance. The leaps, the flexed hands and feet! The strange falls! And the music was foreign.

She didn't belong with these people. They went through the motions with superb accuracy. Some of the pieces were private jokes between them and the panel. Why couldn't she get the punch lines that won glowing approval and smiles?

"I enjoyed your dance."

She turned around. He was the ballet soloist, number seven. His skin could have been a night shadow with no end to its blackness. He had a perfect moustache where most boys had scraggly brown fuzz. His lips were two ripe strips of plum smiling warmly at her. She waited for him to pat his hair, or bat his long eyelashes. He did neither.

She shook her head reluctantly, accepting his compliment.

"You just need some technique. You definitely have the feeling to become a good dancer. Is this your first audition?"

"You can tell."

He laughed with a kindness and maturity that wouldn't allow her to believe that he was fifteen, like her.

"I've been to quite a few auditions," he told her, not intending to boast. "But don't worry. You did fine. You certainly have all the tools. All you need is refinement." He smiled at her again, the way a friend would. "When you're good, they can't say no."

"Thanks," she said, not knowing if he was being smug or kind.

"See you in January."

She felt sick. She had to get out of there in a hurry. She didn't like being surrounded by five hundred Merryls, Cindis, and Jay-Jays. The teachers couldn't have liked her body anyway. She had to get out of the city and climb back into her element. *Ha. Sure. Right. See who in January? Not the kid,* she thought, running down Seventh Avenue. She saw those looks on the other dancers' faces when she finished her audition piece. If she could only get out of the city fast enough she would be all right. She could breathe. Everywhere she turned they were after her. The ballet dancers with the humongous bags, severely clean looks, string bean bodies, and theater accents. Everywhere. The city was full of them.

Joyce hid in the subway.

She didn't begin to feel right until she was actually on her block. Terri and Lynda were turning ropes for Gayle, who jumped double dutch while holding her swollen belly. Baby due January.

Now, those were her home girls. Lynda, Terri, and Gayle, otherwise known as the Southside Crew. Talk about throwing down on some steps! Took second place at the annual talent show at JHS 192, alias the Deuce. Joycie, Terri, Lynda, and Gayle did splits and triple turns. Wouldn't Joyce love to be back at the Deuce with her girls?

"Yo, yo! Can I get a play?"

❧ Seven

Figuring that neither Mays nor Lamstons would call, Joyce began investing in the *Daily News* and sometimes the *Post*. After days of scanning the classifieds, her eyes became well trained in weeding out nonexistent jobs advertised by personnel agencies, or jobs requiring degrees, typing, steno, and experience only. That only left jobs as cab drivers, auto mechanics, bookkeepers, or gal fridays—for none of which she could qualify. Then, just about the time that she usually crumpled the paper and threw it in the trash, an ad caught her eye.

BLOOD DONORS WANTED. CASH PAID.

This was it! This was her part-time job, she decided, ripping the ad from the page. What's a pint? Ten or twenty dollars or more. She could make more money at the blood bank than the ten dollars that Sam gave her. And maybe after seeing her week after week they might just plain old give her a job. Assistant blood technician.

Joyce added up what she would get from donating blood once a week for a few months in the margin of the *News*. She came up with a sum of dance lessons and new clothes. She wouldn't have to ask Minnie for a freakin' dime without her going into a song and dance about saving the money to buy a home. *We got a roof over our heads, don't we? Why do we have to own it? Why are we scrimping just to own four walls? What am I supposed to tell the kids at school? "I may not have really nice clothes but at least I own a house?" Is she mad? But that's OK. With this blood job I can pay for dance lessons and show everybody what I can do. Then we'll see who's the real prima ballerina.*

School was tolerable as long as she avoided Cindi and Jay-Jay and Andre Miller. She learned to spot them first and then turn down another corridor. Standing by herself at the bus stop wasn't so bad either. But having to take class with Cindi and Jay-Jay didn't make things any better, especially with Ms. Sobol using her as the class example of "the Nondancer."

The letter from the conservatory finally came in the mail. She stuffed it in her pocket without saying a word to Minnie. When she got down the block she threw the envelope in a trash can, unopened, without a regret. She refused to give another person the chance to reject her. She knew what was in the letter:

> *Dear Ms. Collins,*
>
> We regret to inform you that your solo was awful. How could you come here and do that spiritual nonsense? We only accept ballet dancers with skinny bodies. Have you ever considered 42nd Street and Eighth Avenue? There's a future in exotic dancing for gals like you.
>
> Don't call us.
>
> > *Sincerely,*
> > *The Real Dancers*

She didn't need their school anyway. She could go to another school and take classes. Their program was probably corny. Probably all ballet.

Joyce avoided the usual crowd at the bus stop. She sat up front with the senior citizens who were bold enough to ride in a busload of high-school kids. She kept her gaze in her paperbacks assigned for English, all the while wondering, *Are they laughing at me?*

Joyce had been planning the day's escape from Cardozo since the third period. When the eighth period bell rang, Joyce ducked out of school through the side door, beating the crowd to the bus stop. From her seat near the driver she prayed for the doors to close, leaving Cindi and Jay-Jay behind, along with the Davis twins and Andre Miller. By now the whole story about how "that big butt girl named Joyce liked Andre and that he said that she couldn't lick his toes if she begged him," was all over school.

Once in Jamaica, she fled the avenue and ambled down Sutphin Boulevard, anticipating her job interview. She played a game of counting graffiti while making mental caricatures of their creators. She made them into frail, bowlegged boys, mainly Puerto Rican, who were either class clowns or incredibly quiet types. It was fascinating. She wanted to catch one at work. Byrd and Motion, obviously partners, dominated Jamaica and Cambria Heights, owning every condemned building, steel roll-up gate, sidewalk, and billboard. Although the other spray-painted names fought hard for recognition, they were clearly a backdrop for the stylish duo.

"Ssssssssss. Say, hey baby. Yo, stuff."

She kept on walking.

"I said, yo, sweetheart. You lookin' so gooood. Uh, can I walk with you?"

"No."

"Yo, yo, yo, yo, yo. Hey. Don't be like that. Uh, what's your name, baby doll."

"Don't worry 'bout my name."

"Yo, like I just got to have some of that," he said, walking all behind her like a dog wagging his tail for some scraps.

"Get offa me! Leave me the hell alone!"

The dog kept barking. "Hey. You think you white or something? You too good to tell me your name? Well look-a-here. You ain't really what's happening no ways, queen. I was just trying to make your day, seeing how badly you needed a lift. You ain't really all that fine."

He made sure he spat his intentions in her ear.

Just keep on moving, Joyce told herself in between long strides, putting enough distance between herself and the dog. He was still telling her about herself, making like he was going to come after her. Joyce had her steel hair pick grasped tightly in her hands. *Better him than me,* she thought.

It wasn't until she was a block from the blood bank that she began to think of the penetration of the needle. The thought of the needle going into her arm made her queasy, and she slowed her pace. Then she thought about seeing the stream of blood leaving her arm and stopped right there. The same sickness sat in her stomach like the time Aunt Em killed the chicken in the backyard and blood gushed out of its dismembered neck. Then the thought of the pain, the needle, and the blood kept rushing at her in cycles.

A wino stumbled out of the swinging glass door, almost knocking her over. She stepped aside so she wouldn't have to touch him. His hair was clumped together like it needed washing and his skin was so dirty that the bright pink Band-Aid on his arm stood out. She looked at his dirty work pants and sweat-drenched T-shirt. The desperation of the situation smacked her hard. Mama would kill her if she saw her at the blood bank. Only down-and-out people and hard-core bums did this—not high-school girls who wanted dance lessons. But it was too late. She was already in the doorway.

The receptionist sitting behind a window gestured Joyce to come up front. Interrupting her telephone conversation, the receptionist hung the receiver over her shoulder and said, "Yes, Miss?"

"I want to donate blood."

"We have to test you first."

"A positive."

"We still have to test you," she insisted, annoyed with the girl who was keeping her from her caller. "How do we know we can use your blood with all these diseases? Junkies and bums come in here all the time, trying to get a few bucks."

While she spoke, Joyce's eyes traveled around the room, stopping at a tray with tubes filled with different solutions. No. She couldn't do it.

But the ten dollars.

No. It will hurt.

But the money.

No, this place is awful.

"Age?"

"Eighteen."

The receptionist's vermilion lips dropped in unconcealed doubt. "Proof?" she challenged.

"What?"

"Do you have a driver's license with you? A birth certificate or something to substantiate your age?"

She had a bus pass and working papers. "I left it at home."

"Come back tomorrow with something. We're open eight to five."

"Sure," Joyce said, relieved. "Tomorrow."

Abandoning her job-hunting composure, Joyce shot through the glass doors, tripping over herself, unable to distinguish her legs from her dance bag. Fear and relief came out of her in short, choppy breaths. Halfway down the block she could still see the blood-filled tubes, smell the sanitary hospital odor, and feel the gritty arm of the bum who had almost brushed up against her.

Ten dollars couldn't mean that much. Somewhere in Jamaica there had to be a job where Joyce could sit, work a fast food counter, or watch someone's kids. Letting someone stick a needle in her arm for money was crazy. Not for new clothes, a leather coat, dance lessons, or anything else.

What if someone had seen her going into the blood bank? It would be all over the school how that big butt girl Joyce was so poor that she had to sell her blood for bus money. She'd never be able to ride the Special again.

Instinct made her hide down a back street to shield herself from any possible onlookers. It would be dark soon. She'd be invisible, free to stroll aimlessly about her South Jamaica without being sifted out.

Da dum dum dum / da dum dum dum / da da dum dum dum

A deep thumping sound pumped through her insides as she walked. She chased it down another side street and followed it up the stairs of a storefront. She knew better than to wander down unfamiliar streets. But she couldn't help herself. Rather, she refused to help herself, putting her life into a young drummer's calling.

❧ Eight

The cracked door let in a breeze of fresh air for the dancers working vigorously in the studio. The drummer sat in the corner, palming his conga skins tenderly. He seemed removed from the dancers and unaware of his command over the spellbound girl isolating her shoulders to his rhythm.

Walls that featured a mural of African deity and dancers in spectacular garb cried out pride and heritage. There were studio portaits from various performances. And there was that long African word that she had seen before. It came back to her. It was that group that she had run into on her way to the transfer auditions. She pried the door open to take in more. There had to be at least twenty dancers, men and women on the floor contracting their torsos and rolling their heads to perfect syncopation of the congas. If Joyce had stopped to look in the mirror, she would have found herself keeping rhythm with the dancers.

"Get dressed! Class started ten minutes ago!" A tall, raisin-colored man yelled at her from across the studio, not once taking his attention away from the class.

She stood dumbfounded, almost afraid to move.

He turned toward her, stopped his class, and folded his arms. "Well?" He looked down at her, an ant in his shadow. "Either take class or leave. We don't allow spectators."

Joyce obeyed as though she had no choice. She scurried down the corridor and found a room with two large burlap screens serving as dividers. She changed quickly into her blue tights and mandarin orange leotard, stuffing her street clothes into her dance bag. When she returned to the studio, room was made for her to squat in between two danceresque girls, one wearing a red Ailey T-shirt and the other, a City College of New York shirt.

"Contract, contract, contract—release! And release, release, release—contract! Left hands on hips and right hands flexed. Twenty times!" he dictated over the steady drumming.

Who was this tall, tall dude? Did he always yell? She had to get her face just right so he wouldn't catch her hissing. She smirked, hearing someone calling his name, Hassan, and she thought Hassan was Swahili for "tall man with a big mouth."

While catching her breath in between exercises, Joyce made a quick scan of the dancers in the studio. Out of the eight men in the class, only three resembled dancers, while the rest, she decided, looked like kung fu warriors. She hoped to see the handsome ballet soloist from the Dance Conservatory auditions, but he wasn't there. She smiled at the toddler sticking close to mama, remembering her visits to the studio with Minnie.

Her gaze fell upon the sculptured body sitting before her in a cardinal red Ailey shirt, matching sweatband restraining her beaded braids. She was toned with long muscles from her neck, upper breasts, and arms down to her legs. She had no stomach. Her face had been carved in fine detail from a smooth black stone. The ripples in her arms made their every gesture that of a danseuse. The bandages wrapped around her toes gave credence to her artistic look.

Joyce made notes on every other female. She watched them dancing with vigor and grace, uninhibited breasts and buttocks jiggling to the demands of the movements. Their shapes and sizes had such variety that she lost her uniqueness in the studio. She was just another dancer.

"You call *those* contractions?" the tall man started. "Lord help us." Nervous snickers came from the rows as he paced. "Some of you I can't even *begin* to describe. . . ." He imitated their lack of energy. "You just get up here and do what you feel regardless of what I ask for. The rest of you—don't let me start." The snickers became uncontained laughter. "Are we dancing or having nervous spasms? You'd never know we had a show coming up." He paced while picking out the guilty faces. "Clarke, demonstrate the pelvic contraction series."

The lithe dancer came willingly to the front of the class and assumed the position for the exercise. The teacher counted as the dancer's body shot up in a V shape, then bounced and released into the floor. He held his position for seven counts, releasing for a one count rest, springing up to hold fourteen. All this he did casually like most people sat at a table and ate a meal.

"I can do that," Joyce muttered under her breath, having an instant dislike for the boy. The show-off.

"Some of you walk in here thinking ethnic gives you license to do any old thing. Just shake booty at random. Hassan won't know the difference." Hassan paused while Clarke basked in his attention. "So . . . let's hold for eight, sixteen, and twenty-four with a perfectly straight back. When I come around the room I want to see beautiful lines, from the head to the sacrum to the toe."

A grave hush fell over the studio. Even the toddler made not a peep. Every dancer wore a look of concentration. Their postures became erect, and their eyes were keenly focused. They continued to lift up from the chest as he paced in between the rows. There was nothing worse than Hassan correcting a student's slouch in the name of dance *and* cultural pride.

The drumming came to an abrupt halt when the drummer tore out of the studio like a fugitive. Everyone continued the exercise as though nothing had happened. With Hassan so near, Joyce didn't dare stop to ask anyone about the drummer.

"Now, ease into your split, bouncing right, left, and center for eight, chests on the floor for that center stretch."

Joyce fell into her split, pleased that she wasn't among the grunters and groaners. She copied the arms of the girl in red, fascinated with the beautiful lines her body made.

"No! Don't just plop into it," Hassan said to Joyce. "Are you a sack of potatoes? Is that what you're going to do on stage? Not with my dances. There are four counts left to this exercise, or can't you count to four?"

Instinct told her to repeat the exercise. No lip.

"Still wrong," he informed her, shifting her so that her upper body was perpendicular. "Now you're stretching."

She certainly was.

"That's good. Very good," he finally complimented her. "We'll make a dancer out of you yet."

She didn't care. She just wanted her legs back.

Finally they came across the floor. The couples dancing across the studio were cheered on by other dancers waiting for their turn to try the combination. It was a matter of finding the beat and jumping into it at the right spot, like jumping double dutch. Every time Joyce neared the front line with her partner she became immersed in the count, feeling every step, every jump, every turn, before Hassan nodded their cue. Pas de bourrées and twinkle toes were never like this, Joyce thought, delighted with this new dance form that communicated so fluently with her body. No one picked apart her every movement or laughed. They cheered. *Cheered.* With the congas drilling inside her, she let the rainbow of leotards whirl around her, never once considering what she looked like, who was looking, and what they were thinking. She just wanted her turn to come up again.

The class ended with thunderous applause.

"Rehearsal from three to six or seven this Saturday."

"He means until about seven or eight," the girl next to Joyce whispered.

"Rehearsal?"

"We're all in the Kwanzaa celebration at Rochdale Center," she replied, unwinding the red band from her braids. "I'm Tamu."

"I'm Joyce," she replied, all the while feeling insecure uttering her plain name in a studio where everyone had exotic names.

"I want to be in the Kwanzaa celebration."

"Everybody's in it. Even the tots. Hassan teaches at the day-care center on Sutphin. That's how he gets so many young mothers in the classes."

The dancers left the studio to form a line at the water cooler in the hallway. Joyce lingered behind to approach Hassan, who was going through some papers on his desk.

"I can't pay for class."

"We'll work something out," he replied. "But first you have to register. Name?"

"Joyce Collins," she told him.

He looked at her as though he might know her, then took it back. He recorded it in a notebook. "Did you ever fill out any Project: Youth employment applications?"

She shook her head no.

"Here." He handed the sheet to her. "In the space that says *agency,* write *Kuji Je Tea Ujana Dance Ensemble.*" He had to chuckle at her attempt to comprehend the foreign words. "It's Swahili for 'pride in youth.' I'll write it," he offered. "And where it says *supervisor,* put my name, Hassan Carter. I'll see you Saturday. And Joyce," he said as she turned away.

"Yes, Mr. Carter?"

"You move well."

She died a thousand times trying to suppress her smile. *Ooooooooooooow girl! Getitgetitgetitgetitgetit— you got it! Ha! You got it like that!*

She was still beaming when she noticed the drummer putting away his conga in a duffel bag. "You're really good," she told him.

He looked up, catching her off guard with the most startling brown eyes.

"Thank you." He lowered his head.

"Do you dance too?"

"No," he replied curtly, apparently offended.

She fumbled. "Anyway," she began backing away, wishing she hadn't said anything to the strange dude, "I like your playing."

She fled behind the burlap screen, anything to get away from him, so she could relish her compliment from Hassan. Everyone was practically naked, washing off in the sink or dashing on powder and smoothing on lotion. Could the boys see through the screen? She wanted to keep her eyes lowered as she hunted for her clothes among the confusion, but she was overcome with temptation to stare at Tamu's body. There. She saw it. It was so, so remarkable. It didn't look real.

"How did you like your first class?" The dancer took Joyce by surprise, reducing her to shame.

Joyce nodded repeatedly until she could assemble the words, "Yeah, pretty good." She pulled her dungarees out of her dance bag, giving them a good shake.

"Aren't you gonna take off your gear? At least your tights!" Tamu protested. "We're all women here. We got what you got, too."

Reluctantly Joyce peeled out of her leotards, then tights, as though it were a painful ordeal. No one paid her any mind. Tamu handed her a wet towel.

"The drummer." Joyce changed the subject. "Is there something wrong with that dude? I mean, is he retarded?"

The thought had never occurred to Tamu and she laughed. "Why do you ask?"

"The way he ran out while we were exercising," Joyce explained, feeling more at ease in the makeshift dressing room, totally amazed that no one wanted to stare at her butt. "And when I spoke to him he looked down like I was diseased."

The twenty-year-old Tamu laughed, charmed by the girl's ignorance. "He's Muslim. He considers you naked and won't look at you in your tights."

Joyce laughed. How stupid.

"You're also a woman," the dancer confided, "and a provocative one at that. One cannot think Allah and watch Joyce dance at the same time."

The other girls laughed.

"Being a woman makes you automatically inferior. Women should make children and not be seen," Tamu explained.

"But why did he run out like that?" Joyce asked.

"To pray before sundown."

"Muslim, huh. Is that why he doesn't watch us dancing?" *Us dancing.* It did sound nice.

"My, my, my. Aren't we curious," Tamu teased.

"Leave her alone," another dancer cut in sympathetically. "Who knows. She just might bring him down to earth with the rest of us infidels."

"Now, now," Tamu admonished, "let the brother be." She turned to Joyce. "I take the Q5. What do you take?"

"I walk. It's not far."

"Are you sure? It's dark out there."

"It's only a few blocks away," Joyce insisted.

"Have it your way. See you Saturday."

The throbbing in Joyce's legs didn't catch up to her until she was midway down the stairs of the building. She was waiting for her legs to give out from under her. But the excitement running around inside made the pain secondary. *He said I move well, move well, move well.* "I mooooove well," she sang in a loud kindergarten singsong.

The drummer wore an army jacket and loose khaki pants. His *taj* fit snugly over his caesar haircut. He looked nothing like the Muslims who stood on corners on Jamaica Avenue, selling oils and incense and passing out literature. He didn't wear all white like them or have any facial hair. His brows were too serious for his sparkling brown eyes, eyes that belonged to a springbok. His face was unblemished by a typical hardness worn by most guys his age. He wasn't especially tall, and had just enough chest to be considered somewhat manly. Everything said seventeen.

She waltzed by him, hoping for his attention and to let him know she wasn't intimidated.

"A woman shouldn't be out by herself after sundown."

"I'm not scared of anything out here. This is my neighborhood."

He had expected her attitude to be as such.

"If you respected yourself as a woman you would not walk the streets alone at night."

Twice regarded as a woman.

"So."

"I'll walk you home."

She tried to think of something to say to the Muslim but nothing worked in her mind. *Sell any incense lately? Damn. Gayle Whitaker was all of fourteen, pregnant, had a man, and I can't get past hello.*

He walked more slowly than she did, making the silence between them that much more noticeable. She was so used to rushing to avoid people eyeing her, that walking slowly with a boy was uncomfortable. Sam had driven her in his car around town. Walking with a boy for the first time was different. Just think. To anyone who saw them they were a dude and his lady strolling along in the moonlight.

"I am J'had Al Mu'min. It means 'one who struggles and believes.' "

She laughed inwardly at his manner and wanted to say "I am Joyce Collins. It means 'one who is daughter of Minnie Mouse.' " Instead she attempted his name.

"Ja—what?"

"J'had Al Mu'min."

"Right," she said, refusing to pronounce it. *Tamu, Hassan, J'had.* Whatever happened to *Tyrone* and *Sharon*? "So what do you believe?"

"That I shall bear witness to no one but Allah, all praises be unto His name, that Muhammad is His true prophet, and that I shall study and follow the readings of the Holy Quran and practice the Five Pillars of Faith," he recited.

66

"Oh yeah, I almost forgot," she interjected, dismissing his speech altogether. "My name is—"

"Joyce," he told her.

"How did you know that?"

"I heard you talking to Brother Hassan."

"You don't like my name, do you?"

He paused. "It is just a sound against my ear with no more meaning than the word *sand*. It says nothing about who you are, what your admirable traits are and where you came from, your history—absolutely nothing. A meaningless sound: *Joyce.*"

"At least I know who the hell I am. I am Joyce Alicia Collins. I was born in Queens General Hospital. I live in a house, Southside action, you dig?" she retorted, her neck doing a wild snake dance. "And I don't have to change my name to be somebody!" She burned her sneakers into the concrete, determined to leave him standing there.

He caught up as though she hadn't moved at all.

"South Jamaica isn't where you're from. That's where you live," he told her. "You say it as though you're proud to live in that slave environment that someone stuck you in."

Oh no. He done did it now, 'cause he insulted the best that Minnie could do for herself and her daughter.

"Well who the hell are you? You live in some mansion?"

"That's right, Southside. Get vulgar. Wanna throw down next? What's wrong with you black women? You can't get your point across without getting loud! You women cry respect, but are you worthy?"

She sucked her teeth and flicked her hand, and if he got caught by her backhand that would have been OK.

"How come you know so much about being a freakin'

woman? You ain't no woman. You don't know what we put up with just trying to get to the store and back without some dog gettin' all in our faces like we public property, or gettin' loud—ready to fight because we don't give our names! School me, baby. What do you know about being a woman?"

Please don't let me cry. I can't let no one see me cry, she prayed over and over, feeling the tears welling up in her eyelids.

They turned down South Road. She spotted two guys with spray cans and wanted to stop and watch them apply their art. If she could only make out the red and black markings on the condemned laundromat. He noticed her stretching her neck to get a good look.

"That's why you can't be out by yourself at night."

She sighed, annoyed with his concern. Like he's her moms.

"They're only ghostwriters doin' their thang," she informed him.

"Do you know why they do that? Deface property?"

"Speak plain, Jane," she said. How could *he* possibly understand ghostwriters? "Why?" And she rolled huge cow eyes to the sky.

"For people like you who wonder who they are," J'had said.

"And you know all about it," Joyce replied.

"Alias Li'l Alcatraz."

"Wow. I know you! You're under the overpass, and the Long Island Rail Road, and over in the handball court at Liberty Park." Joyce went from sarcasm to awe.

"And behind the 103rd Precinct, and all over Andrew Jackson and the courtyard at Sutphin."

She was indeed impressed. There was finally something worth liking about him. "What made you stop?"

"Almost losing my life just to get my graffiti up in the subway at Parsons Boulevard. I was with my boys," he reflected, his voice changing, "and we was fiiiiired up."

Joyce looked at him hard, trying to picture him as a get-high type.

"It was twelve-fifteen. The next E train wasn't due for another ten minutes. I jumped down into the tracks and started doing my logo. Silver and black. I was just about to finish my z. I didn't want to mess up the curve on the end. That was my trademark. I could hear the train coming. Something wouldn't let me leave it alone. I just kept at it. At the same time I was paralyzed. Once I saw the lights I felt death coming at me. It felt so real, so clear, that I could feel the cold metal, my bones crushed. Then a thought came to me. I just couldn't do anything to hurt my moms. Just seeing cops explaining my death would kill her. In a millisecond I heard a thousand screams all coming from my moms who had to identify my remains, and that's when I jumped up on that platform. To this day I can't remember jumping. Me and the boys laughed it up good that night, drinking Olde English '800.' Joyce, when I got home I couldn't even sleep. I just cried all night. That's when I knew I had to make a change. I had to do this," he gestured to his cap. "I got humble real quick and submitted my life to Allah."

"So how long you been a Muslim?" This time there was genuine interest in her query.

"A while," he responded, making it seem like a few months.

"And what does your mama say about you dressing all fun— different," she caught herself.

"She said God would punish me. Then she wouldn't speak to me for days. She's Baptist. Her mind is closed. And she gets mad when I start talking to her about submitting, especially with my brothers and sisters around. 'Junior, don't be puttin' that Mooslim talk in their heads. They Christians.' "

She laughed at his imitation.

"But she doesn't know," he said sadly. "I did it for her, and Allah, of course."

Joyce could see her house. Minnie was sitting in the front room straining her neck to see out of the window.

"That's my mother," Joyce warned. It finally dawned on her that she had not called home. And the time! "Thank you for walking me home," she told him, stepping up her pace, as if to beg him not to follow. He understood and remained on the corner until she was inside her house.

"Girl, where have you been?" Minnie didn't raise her voice. She didn't have to. Her words meant business.

Joyce panicked. "I-I-I was at the studio."

"What studio? I don't know nothing 'bout no studio. Who was that nigger with you?" She got up, meaning to tower over the daughter whom she had to look up to. "Fifteen and already in the streets carrying on."

Joyce was completely flustered, unable to speak or pronounce the name of the dance group, let alone J'had's name. "Here, Mama," she said, presenting the Project: Youth application hoping it would add credence where she drew a blank. "They let me take classes there for free, and—"

"Who was that boy?"

"J'had." She forgot the rest. "The drummer. He was walking me home so I would be all right."

"OK. It's late." Minnie finally calmed down. After all, Joyce had never given her any real trouble. "Get upstairs and do your homework."

That was Minnie's word. Joyce climbed the stairs.

He thought of her as a woman. He had the prettiest eyes. Li'l Alcatraz himself.

Minnie stared out of the raised window hoping the night air would clear the devil from her head. She didn't mean to pounce on Joyce. It was an instinctive reaction. All of a sudden, the words she had rehearsed for her mother-daughter sit-downs were nonsense gathered from "Father Knows Best."

Joyce leaned against the window in her room. He was long gone. She closed the blinds and moved away, thinking that Mama was mad enough to kill and that his eyes had touched her eyes. And they were brown. Like hers.

❧ Nine

The bare-chested overseer strode between the rows of straddled dancers, pounding a wooden pole with bells. When Joyce felt the heat of his presence she immediately centered her body, lifted her head, added more point or flex to her toes. Anything so he would overlook her.

Hassan was not concerned with a student's personal hang-ups and had no qualms about physically shifting a body into place. Joyce knew better than to draw back, talk back, or suck her teeth when he approached her with corrections.

"Are you going to do that on stage? Look at everyone else's stomach. Why should yours be the only one hanging out? Are you pregnant?"

He stood over her, daring her to utter the sound or flinch the muscle that would destroy her alignment.

Occupied with her own form, Tamu offered Joyce no sympathy or encouraging looks as she usually did. J'had's gaze had long strayed out of the window, and he was thinking those Muslim thoughts.

The conspiratorial air was thickening. As far as

Joyce was concerned, everyone was a part of it and she was the outsider. Everyone seemed to work quietly, knowing something was to happen.

Hassan finally abandoned Joyce and worked in the corner where the drummer sat where he could develop a dance phrase. The class looked on, trying to decipher his underplayed gestures. Joyce remained puzzled, trying to pick up on whatever the class was attuned to.

Satisfied with the combination he had pieced together, Hassan nodded to himself, then to J'had, who responded with a slightly picked-up rhythm.

"Women on the floor. Men over to the side."

As the women assembled into four rows, Hassan instructed them to watch him. Joyce felt comfortable in the second row behind Tamu. She could see what was going on and also be seen.

The half movements came to life in Hassan's torso and arms like undulating smoke wafting through cool air. Joyce never thought he could actually move. Teachers didn't dance. Teachers yelled and poked at those who could. Then it dawned on her while taking in his control and ease: He had an even greater passion for movement than she did and she had miles to catch up. Was it possible that old Ms. Sobol could dance too?

He broke the routine into two counts of sixteen. When he felt that he had taught it sufficiently, he asked, "Everbody got it?" as though he'd taught a nursery rhyme to collegians. They more or less nodded. "OK. . . . Let's see everyone, then row one, two, and so on."

Joyce did not notice Hassan picking apart the dancers row by row. Her head was too far gone in the rigors of rolling and snapping. This was even better than going across the floor. She trusted the combination completely. As she came in on his count, the room began to spin. The background swirled and it was just she and the path J'had made for quick feet. Joyce took control of the floor space; she isolated contractions and ripples with definition and clarity. Where others would hesitate to ask if the body could go so far, she was already there.

"Let me see you,"—he pointed decisively—"you,"—thoughtfully—"and you"—smiling. "Everyone else can sit."

The dancers cleared the floor reluctantly.

"You." He cornered Joyce who was preparing to sit down. "Where are you going?"

"Who me?" Joyce asked without a clue that she had been selected.

Hassan motioned impatiently for Joyce to get in position. Tamu and another chosen dancer were already waiting for the count of one. Joyce ran to her spot on the floor.

"And!" he shouted before she had a chance to become apprehensive. She felt each movement as she jumped in, seeing their actual shapes an instant before the execution.

The class applauded on the sixteenth count.

"Let me see Joyce," Hassan told the other dancers, who took their places on the side. "Add this." It was a traveling motion. She seemed to know it from somewhere. Food for her supple torso. "Take that sixteen counts and repeat the first phrase."

They were all looking at her. The entire class. Tamu. Clarke. J'had. And for the first time it felt wonderful to have so many eyes upon her. Not because her tail was round or because they were waiting to laugh. But because she was the dancer to watch. She didn't want to shrink away from their waiting eyes: Joyce wanted to dance for them.

Once the drumming started, Joyce's imagination let her become anyone she wanted to be. She felt her arms and torso telling the story of the river maiden gathering cascades of water. She moved fluently within the phrases, cleverly scooping water into calabash gourds where the others danced the phrase as a simple arm flutter—not like Joyce the River Maid raising the Volta! Balancing the imaginary gourd on her head, she gave richness to a dry earth and gave dance to a cheering studio.

Joyce whirled swiftly around the down of the tempo and finished a hair of a second before the final count. The class roared. Hassan only nodded, confirming what he had known all along.

"Men, take the floor."

The eight male dancers took their places in two rows. The reluctant ones hiding in the back were urged up front by Hassan's insistent stare.

Joyce staggered to where the females squatted, affected by a combination of exhaustion, dizziness, and thrill. She was dragged down playfully by Tamu, who ran her fingers in Joyce's sweating and curly mop, praising Joyce for her down-to-earth style.

"I didn't know rehearsal was gonna be like this!" Joyce exclaimed in between breaths. "Am I gonna solo every night like that?"

"My child," Tamu began, somewhat amused. "This isn't rehearsal. This is audition."

"Audition?"

Another dancer laughed at the lost girl. "You just got the lead in the *Kwanzaa Suite*. That's all."

"No!"

"You have the duet," Tamu explained, cautioning her to lower her voice with a raised finger over her lips. "The boy who gets picked will be your partner. But personally," she whispered, "we all know who that will be."

"Clarke Kent," the other dancer rejoined snidely.

"Well, he does deserve it," Tamu admitted with that sense of fairness inherent in her nature. "But, I think Hassan should start paying some attention to Scott, or that one with the nice extension, before Bernice Johnson or Gloria Jackson gets them. Clarke gets a lot of play but these other guys shouldn't be ignored. The other guys just might lose interest and we need all the fellas we can get. But that's studio politics." She had to shake her braids on the truth. "Anyway," Tamu resumed on a pleasant note, "I'm glad you got it. I danced the part three years straight. All power to ya."

Studio politics? Joyce had enough people hating her at school. She was just beginning to feel at home with the workshop. Before she knew it they would all hate her too.

"I never really danced before," Joyce blurted out. "I was in a talent show in junior high, but we was just B-boying and doing free style. I mean, not really dancing like with technique."

"Hassan will guide you. You have fast pickup and you can move."

Another girl gave an encouraging nod.

"But I—"

"Joyce. There are a lot of girls who have been coming here for years working their tails off hoping to be noticed. You come in off the street, out of the blue, and you're already Hassan's girl. Now, we're not particularly vicious, but break your leg and see how fast we jump for your part. Sure, there's some jealousy, but you have to deal with it. The minute you act like you can't handle it the attitudes will fly up. Don't be scared no one won't like you. Not when you can dance like that."

Six males were immediately seated. Joyce got a good

look at Clarke and Scott. She noted Clarke's apparent confidence and ease of movement. Her first impressions were strong. She didn't like him at all. But Scott had a different way about him. His massive chest and solid features were built to accommodate her. Scott charged through the routine like a soldier, determined to get the duet. Not with the same finesse as his opponent but with strength and control. Joyce leaned toward Scott's aggressive appeal and was turned off by the aloof Clarke. But Scott's valiant fight for the lead was in vain. Clarke's effortless dance confirmed that the role was his.

After the auditions, Joyce undressed fully, relieved to peel away the sticky leotards and tights. She rubbed a wet towel in the creases of her arms and between her breasts and plastered another on her throbbing thighs. The idea of street clothes was inconceivable. Tamu was totally dressed except for lacing up her boots.

"Joyce, concentrate on your extensions. You're not turning out. But don't worry. We'll work on it tomorrow."

"Leave Joyce alone. She gets into it," another defended.

Tamu ignored the interloper. "Do you take ballet?"

"Well," Joyce said, "they're making me take this jive technique class in school, but the teacher can't dance. And that class is so dry."

"But you need it," Tamu said while lacing up her boots. "So you don't like ballet. That's why you're afraid of Clarke."

"I'm not scared of him."

"Let me tell you. Clarke is gonna eat you up alive on that stage. So I advise you to get whatever that schoolteacher's got to give you. Believe me. I know."

"Yeah. Right. Sure."

"Other than that you did pretty good. See ya."

Joyce dressed quickly. J'had was downstairs.

"I got the duet! I'm the African queen!" She let it out as though she had been saving it for him alone.

He nodded.

"You don't like it?"

"I'm not the one that you have to please in the end," he told her with judgment apparent.

"What?"

"When you pass from this life I hope Allah is pleased with what you have done."

She waited for him to continue, all the while angry that he wanted no part of her joy.

"Those who know of Allah and refuse to humble themselves and submit before Him will burn up in the hell fire."

"And I'm going to hell because I dance?" Joyce asked, not taking him seriously.

"Exactly."

She sucked her teeth and flicked her hand up in the air, letting her bangles clang. "You're just saying that to scare me."

"I hope you *are* scared. That's good. Allah means serious business," he told her. "Sister, Allah wants you to prepare and submit before Him."

"Allah. Allah. Everything is Allah with you. Why can't you be a regular dude?"

"Like the street thugs trying to get a little tail?"

"No. Like an everyday dude enjoying life."

"In the Nation of Islam I have more freedom than you, in your world. All that's taboo, I can live without."

"Taboo?"

"Smoke, drink, party, curse, fornicate."

"Forni-whaaat?

"Fornicate. Sex without the benefit of marriage," he explained to a most ignorant Nubian woman.

"Well, what if you're with your lady and you have the

urge—and I know you be getting urges. You ain't Superman. Then what?"

"Suppress it," he said automatically. "Take a shower. Do something else to release the thoughts from my mind. Meditate."

She thought about the intensity of her feelings. There wasn't that much meditation and showers in the world.

"But don't you ever want to just do it? I mean, like what if you're really all"—she paused searching for a delicate phrase—"all worked up and you just have to get some. I mean, what if—"

"I'll find a wife and get married," he responded ever so quickly to save his ears from being offended.

"I can't wait that long," she told him, " 'cause I'm a woman and I need loving. Just waitin' for the right dude."

He was momentarily pleased by her answer. She was a virgin. There was time. Even better, there was hope.

"That's a start," he told her with great plans in mind for her. "One day I'd like to read a passage from the Quran to you, sister."

"Quran, Saran. Everything is Quran with you. That Quran can't say how I danced."

"Are you asking me?"

She nodded.

"Sister, you move nice."

She smiled as though she had won a victory.

"But," he interjected, "I still don't think that should be done in public."

"Why? What's wrong with it?"

"Sister, don't you feel any shame, half-naked, shaking parts of your body that no one should notice? A Muslim woman would never allow herself to be displayed like that."

"Do I look like a Muslim woman to you?"

"No. But your time will come. Just like mine did. You will submit."

"Yeah. Right. Sure." She dismissed him. "Show you what you know. That's art that I'm doing. Primus technique. The movement of African kings and queens," she recited from one of Hassan's many lectures. "I'm not just shaking my body at random, you know."

"No decent Muslim woman would exhibit herself like that," he insisted.

"How can you say that when you drum for me? Can't you feel what's going on between us when you're playing and I'm dancing? Don't it feel spiritual?" she implored him with huge eyes.

He followed the development of her every word as they formed on her lips. He was hung up on her helpless anger.

"It's a job," he explained. "I take karate at the center in exchange for drumming for Hassan."

Didn't he know he just hurt her? And after making her dance?

"So Allah lets you drum, but I can't dance."

"Men don't fall to the same temptations as a woman."

"Forget it. Forget you."

"Your mother's waiting for you. *As salaam alaikum.*"

"Sayonara, Charlie Brown."

She could barely say a decent "Hi, Ma" when she got in the door. She burned from the inside, but anger was only part of it. She plunked down on her bed and thought she would catch fire.

"Damn," she told her poster of Michael looking sweet and inaccessible on her wall, "how come all of the truly fine guys are either taken, gay, or Muslims?"

✿ Ten

Joyce earned her first break while Hassan rehearsed the male chorus. The other girls sat under the water cooler, chatting noisily and showing off their steps. Clarke occupied the center mirror, watching himself pirouette. Tamu and another dancer labored on a class project at the far end of the studio.

Joyce watched as Tamu picked apart the phrase that resembled leapfrog in alternating fast and slow motion. Joyce didn't like it, didn't understand it, and didn't want to, taking immediate offense at the strange concoction that defied feeling and rhythm. Tamu explained the assignment as a study in dynamics and shape in 3/4 time using the Cunningham idiom. Joyce nodded in spite of her lack of comprehension. It wasn't dance to Joyce. How could Tamu do it as though she enjoyed it?

Joyce felt that apparent exclusion which set her apart from Tamu, Clarke, Cindi and Jay-Jay, Merryl, and the ballet soloist from the conservatory. They were on one level of stair steps and she was on another. Even when she looked toward the earthy Tamu for some reassurance, Tamu was into her work, actually enjoying it.

It frightened her more than ballet.

A roll of thunder from the congas brought her focus back to the male chorus. Scott predominated in the foreground, while the lesser dancers faded against his forceful presence. Right away she picked up on his desire and frustration, all compelling him to move the way he did. She knew that mixture all too well and wanted to dance with him because of it.

Clarke darted in and out of her side vision. There was no dealing with someone who didn't put his body into ethnic the way she did. And there was just no getting used to someone who had to be in the mirror for every count.

It was too much. Joyce had to get out of that studio. She had had enough studio jealousy to last a year. How was she supposed to enjoy her solo when the girls all whispered about her, pointing out everything she did wrong. "They're just jealous," Tamu would say casually as though Joyce simply had to get used to it. A dancer's life, Tamu called it. And Clarke? Who was he? Baryshnikov's brother? And then Hassan rode her hard. *I thought he liked me.*

"*As salaam alaikum,*" J'had greeted her as she stepped from behind the curtain. She wrinkled her face, clearly not comprehending. "It's a greeting. You're supposed to say *wa alaikum salaam.* Peace be with you also."

"Oh." She refused to try it.

They turned down a different street than their usual route. Joyce suspected it was so their walk would be longer, and they could talk more.

"Can I ask you something?"

This is it! He's gonna ask me to be his lady.

"Yes?" she managed softly, as the excitement raced around in her head.

"Sister, why do you dress like that?" He looked at her sternly. "Your pants are so tight, they show off everything you have. There is no mystery to your form."

"Damn. You'd think I was naked," she snapped.

"A man has only to look at you to see what you have." He sensed her hurt feelings and paused. He tried a different way. "Sister, your body should be a precious gem, reserved for your husband's eyes alone."

"So what do you want me to do? Wear a sack? People will look at me like I'm crazy."

"How do they look at you now? Every time I see you you're wearing those tight dungarees."

"Well, I don't have money to be buying all new clothes."

"If you come to the mosque you'll meet sisters who will show you how to wear a *khimar,* have respect for yourself, and make yourself pleasing to Allah. Don't worry about how others will look at you. They're not interested in your true beauty. But as a Muslim woman in a *khimar,* you'll be the most beautiful of Allah's creations."

"Suppose I do all this," she said coolly, trying to slick off his association of beauty with Joyce, "I still want to dance."

He shrugged as though all that he had said had fallen upon deaf ears. "I want. I want. It's not what you and I want. It is what Allah wants for us."

"Well, Allah ain't here. We are."

"Through Islam you will learn that Allah is in all things."

Joyce loved watching J'had get all worked up about being a Muslim. He was so serious. Not like the clowns on the Special or that Tinkertoy Clarke.

"So why don't you come to the mosque and bear witness."

"Do what?"

"Take your *shahaad'ah.*"

"You mean do the Muslim pledge? Is you crazy? My moms would kill me."

"Joyce, when a person submits to Allah, he is at peace. It means that he has accepted Allah's will."

She resisted the urge to say something smart. "But I want to dance."

Hardheaded, he thought. "If you had to choose between your God and dance, you would choose dance?"

"Yes," she declared without thinking.

"Well, Sister No-name, Sister Southside, Sister Dance. I hope to see you prancing in the heavens when Judgment Day comes."

"Suppose I submit. Will you watch me dance?"

"Ego, sister," he said, still not giving up. "You have a tremendous ego. God gave you that talent and you should give it to Him, not me."

"But I want to give it to you." She wandered far from dance.

"Joyce, don't say that," he warned.

Her hand went to touch his. He drew back, scorched by fire.

"Sister, you can't do that."

"All I did was touch your hand. I don't have fleas, you know."

"A woman shouldn't just touch a man. It arouses his feelings," he admitted.

"Did I rape you? I just wanted to hold hands. That's all."

"Joyce, I'm trying to respect you. Why won't you respect me?"

Joyce didn't want to hear anything about respect and

ways. She craved tenderness. He was so close. Didn't he like her?

"I know the deal. You don't have to worry about walking me home or being seen with me or holding hands with me. You're like the kids at school. Talking about my clothes and whatnot. But that's cool. I don't need you for no friend."

"I wasn't snapping on your clothes to hurt you."

"Yeah. Right. Sure."

"Joyce, I have feelings for you. I can't begin to share them with you without the intent of marriage."

"Can't I just be your lady?"

He wanted to laugh at her but he didn't. "We don't have ladies and girlfriends. We have wives."

"I'm too young to get married. I just need loving."

"I could love you, Joyce. As a Muslim husband loves his wife. Just come with me to the mosque. Submit."

"Submit?"

"Bear witness to Allah."

"There's Mama. I have to go," she told him quickly, grateful to see her mother. "Salaam shazaam."

Minnie had been sitting in the window talking to herself when she saw Joyce come down the block with that boy. *That boy.* She poured the last of the gin into her glass and filled the ashtray with another crushed cigarette butt.

Without warning she flamed up into rage. A rage brought on by fear and knowing. The kind that consumed her when her ten-year-old girl was sent home from school with her first sanitary napkin. The kind that made Minnie slap Joyce when she accused the stepdaddy of looking at her all funny.

Seeing them walking together, all slow and in the dark, ground into her womb. Even in the dark she knew that boy was tall and handsome and stirring feelings between her baby's legs and she hated him. That boy. Hated that boy for taking her baby. Hated that boy for making her little girl a woman. Hated that boy for doing to her baby what Eddie had done to her sixteen years ago. And seeing Eddie today, with his wife and family, after sixteen years, brought her anger to the surface—put her in a rage aimed at Joyce and that boy.

"Mama? Are you all right?" Joyce entered the living room cautiously, not used to seeing her mother like that.

"How come that boy run off when he see me?"

"He's not running, Mama."

Minnie grunted. "How come he don't speak? Ain't he got no upbringing?"

"He got upbringing. He's really nice."

Minnie laughed. "I know all about nice boys. They'll tell you anything and throw you away when they finished."

It was the gin talking. Mama didn't mean that. She didn't even know J'had.

"Don't you be no fool. He only want one thing," Minnie said, pointing her finger.

"He want to marry me," Joyce said, eager to prove Minnie wrong.

"Marry you? And live where? Support how? He's living home with Mama. He get you pregnant and then what? He'll take off, act like he don't know you, and find him a society gal to marry. While they living high, you'll be stuck with a baby that looks like him."

"Mama, he does love me. He wants to marry me."

Minnie's laugh was stretched out and evil. Joyce didn't know the woman.

Joyce sucked her teeth. "You don't know nothin'."

"I don't? I don't?" The words heightened Minnie's agitated state. "How do you think you got here? You think

I wanted you? Eddie left 'causa you." Her voice trembled. She stepped toward Joyce with her back hunched. "I give up everything 'causa you. Dance, school, parties, Eddie. I had no kinda life 'causa you. You think I wanted you?"

Joyce left her mother screaming in the living room and slammed her door. She didn't care if Minnie knocked down the door and tried to beat her. What could Minnie do to her? J'had was the only person in the world who really cared. Mama was just losing her mind. How could Mama say those things? What could Mama know about love? What did Mama know about J'had's true love? What did Mama know 'bout anything?

Joyce threw some of her belongings into a shopping bag. Minnie would be sorry. Come Sunday, Joyce was going to the mosque to submit and marry J'had and leave Minnie by her damn self.

Joyce opened her closet to pull out the rest of her things. That's when she saw the brand-new leather coat from Mama hanging up in the center. She touched it. It was real leather. It was baaaaad. It was . . . thrown underneath the bed.

✖ Eleven

The next morning the leather coat sleeve sticking out from underneath Joyce's bed pleaded to be rescued and placed on a hanger. Joyce ignored it, going for her brown vinyl jacket. She pulled her arms through the sleeves in an exaggerated effort, to prove that she didn't need anyone's leather coat. She flung her dance bag over her shoulder and left the closet door wide open so Minnie could see exactly what she thought of the leather coat.

Minnie called in sick to work to take care of her throbbing head. She wanted to be forgiving and made eggs, toast, and tea for her daughter. But when she saw the girl bouncing defiantly down the stairs in that beat-up jacket, she pursed her lips, taking back her forgiveness.

"Sit yourself down and eat this food."

"I ain't hungry."

"Ain't asked you if you hungry. Sit down."

Joyce knew Mama's limit and obeyed. Her slouch and vacant stare remained as protests.

"I saw your daddy yesterday when I was buying the

coat. He was with his wife and two little boys. He said hello, introduced me to his wife. I'm one of his old classmates. Ha ha. You should have seen him. Designer suit on him. Wife had a fur coat. Dig it. Full-length fox. Real pearls. Two little boys wearing real leather coats. But Mama was cool. I played it off," Minnie said. "It just hurt to see the life I could have had. And when I saw you with that boy, I saw myself at fifteen. And no mama wants her baby to be hurt or make mistakes."

Joyce was determined to stay slouched and unmoved. She couldn't let Minnie know how much a daddy meant to her. Eddie's picture had been pressed inside Minnie's Bible, and Joyce as a little girl would steal it and hide in the bathroom with his image. She'd trace his nose, his smile, and wish real hard so he would come back for Mama's sake and for her sake so she'd be Daddy's little girl.

"Now get on to school and study your lesson. Leave that Muslim boy alone," Minnie warned. "Don't be in a hurry to end your life."

It wasn't going to work, Joyce thought. Minnie was just trying to break her. Make her cry or something. *Well, I'm too grown to cry and I don't need no daddy. Got me a man.*

Mama's words bounced around the four walls, then fell flat. What did Mama know about being fifteen and needing love?

Joyce cut Dance II, geometry and homeroom, and hung out by the side entrance of the school. When she got cold enough she went inside well after the fourth-period bell had rung.

The hallways were cool, meant for roaming. Joyce discovered that early in the term. She didn't like the so-called better school or her honors classes. The Jewish boys told jokes that the whole class laughed at that she never got at all. Being alone in those classes made her the experiment, and she wasn't about that. She stayed out in the halls until they changed her program from honors to regular. She didn't mind. Not really. At least now there was someone else to cast are-they-for-real? glances to.

Ducking under the stairways or going down to the basement was her way of escaping from those people who had to have tans during the winter, had to touch her hair, had to know exactly what she meant by this or that—then run it in the ground.

Twenty minutes remained to the period. Another girl walking aimlessly down the hall nodded to Joyce as they passed each other. They spoke the hall walker's code. *I'm on the outside, too.*

The girl made a fast break in the opposite direction and down the stairs before the truant officer spotted her. Joyce cut left to the dance studio. She stopped running when she heard Ann Sobol's voice over the delicate tapping of piano keys.

Merryl was rehearsing her solo for the performance. It never occurred to Joyce that Ms. Sobol would find fault with Merryl. But Joyce studied Merryl, the dancer, not the show-off who was always twirling in front of the mirror. Joyce stood quietly, recording everything—the clean distinction of every step, the high feeling in the chest, the eyes that opened and focused. But ballet? How do you feel ballet?

"No! No! This is supposed to be playful! You're making it look like something very hard to do." The dance instructor stood over her, disregarding Merryl's exasperation. "Again. Play with it. It's fun," she insisted, demonstrating with swift glides and quick prances. "You're a princess on her sixteenth birthday. Come now. Glissade, glissade, glissade, piqué . . ."

Joyce mouthed the instruction along with the breaks in the piano rhythm. In her head she was marking the steps, not yet with arms, but just enjoying the silly little things that the feet did. It was bouncy. It was fun. She added the arms and a double piqué turn and oh! ballet was wonderful!

"Hey, you're good."

One of the girls from the show had been watching her from the stairway. "Why aren't you in the show?"

Joyce darted up the stairs.

The combination of tempers flying and irons pressing contributed to the steamy air backstage. Pecking hens in costume jewelry and leotards fretted over hairpieces that wouldn't stay up, mismatched slippers, and steps forgotten. Every ten seconds a prima donna sobbed, "I'm not doing it!"

Through the thick of it, Ann Sobol strolled about coolly, clipboard in hand, checking the lighting and sound, examining the marks on the stage floor, soothing ruffled egos, and rescuing Prince Florimund from Sheilah, who threatened to "jack him up if he didn't act right."

First, the blue-eyed blond boy had to recover from being called a nigger by the lanky black girl. Then he whispered to the director, "Ann, I told you to get professional stage hands instead of these"—he referred to Sheilah.

Ms. Sobol uttered a soothing word to calm the only tenth-grade boy brave enough to wear tights. She admonished Sheilah and that was that.

Chiffons, crepes, and satins were shoved under Joyce's nose by desperate ballerinas who needed them back in a hurry, unwrinkled and unburnt. Whether she had planned to or not, Joyce became involved with the production of *Sleeping Beauty*. She became vital to the dancers who needed her approving smile as they modeled the outfits that she had repaired and ironed. It wasn't that bad. Working costumes with Sheilah earned her a good seat in the wings and the title of Wardrobe Mistress adjacent to her name in the program.

Even so, a bothersome twinge trickled down her back with every button sewn and every wrinkle pressed out. She wanted to wear the costumes, not mend them. She wanted to be onstage, not backstage. All of that flutter and fury was so appealing. She wanted to be in it, if only to be one of the courtesans who merely posed, smiled, and curtsied.

"I can't remember the step."

"Does this look right to you?"

"Chassé, two, three . . ."

"Just fake it. Jump when they jump."

"Look at her. She's gonna mess it up. I don't know why she's doing the part."

"Sobol's pet."

"I can't get this cabriole thing."

"Just keep smiling and move your arms. The audience won't know."

Merryl was stationed in a corner doing toe exercises. Her dinner consisted of an apple, two wheat crackers, and a bottle of Perrier. Glued to a centerfold of Patricia McBride in *Dancemagazine,* she calmly dismissed the panic going on around her. She couldn't be bothered. Her satin bodice and chiffon skirt were cloaked by a terry bathrobe. Merryl herself was shielded by her own sense of cool. She was prepared to perform despite the lack of professionalism in the production, and sat erect, waiting for her interview with the *Daily News.*

Cindi and Jay-Jay were hunched over their makeup mirrors, whispering about the redhead who would play the queen. She was out to make them look tacky by overdoing the regalia in her minor role. "The only reason she's doing a mime character is because she can't dance."

"Right."

Cindi and Jay-Jay's heads bobbed up and down in search of another cast member to discuss. They were not going to be outdone by anyone—Merryl included. While everyone else applied their dime store Max Factor, Cindi and Jay-Jay were armed with the real stage pancake.

"Why are *they* the only ones with crow's feet and highlighters? Everyone should have them!" Prince Florimund demanded.

Ann Sobol appeased him with a compliment that worked for the moment, and walked away without exploding. He was the only boy who could lift his head, point his toes, and wear tights at the same time. She was at his mercy.

The curtain opened for the first act. Joyce had to see what was so special about this show that it could be ruined by her round tail. Joyce and Sheilah ran to the wings and squatted at the curtain's edge. The two girls had made a pact to snap at anyone who messed up, or even better, tripped.

Merryl, a satin butterfly, made her entrance and was greeted by applause from the audience. She bourréed between lords and ladies with gaiety pasted on so thick that it would take sad soap to wash it from her face.

Then Joyce's classmate disappeared and a princess in Merryl stepped forward. Joyce became entranced by the delicate, flowing arms, the wit of youthful play, the gazellelike legs that darted through the air, slicing it at whim. Joyce felt every correction that Ann Sobol had

93

ever made on her body all coming to life in Merryl's lifted head, expanded chest, and swift limbs. She understood the meaning of line. She felt the divinity of the center in Merryl's pirouettes. And then it dawned on her about Ms. Sobol:

She doesn't hate me. She just wants me to be good.

Joyce got up early in order to sneak into the kitchen without arousing her mother. She pulled a hot comb through the roots of her bushy hair. When the evidence was cleaned from the smoking hot comb, she crept back upstairs. There, she parted her hair down the center, weaving a thick cornrow from crown to nape on both sides. The thick braids resembling baked challah loaves were pinned by ivory-colored combs.

She stared in the mirror and admired her artwork. When she was through appraising the tidy cornrows, she stopped at that detail that she hid from. Her face. She had a rather sweet face. A smooth, cinnamon-brown face with dark eyes, a blunt Bantu nose, and perfectly defined full lips. She had her daddy's face.

"Well, check her out," Jay-Jay whispered to Cindi, pointing to a different Joyce approaching them at the bus stop. They managed to get in a few more comments and giggles as she neared them.

"The show was good," Joyce told them. "I liked it."

They nodded in agreement, taking in the much-awaited feedback long after the applause had died down.

"I'm in a show," Joyce volunteered. "I'm dancing a lead opposite this professional dancer named Clarke. He's been in all kinds of Broadway productions," she boasted, hating herself for depending on Clarke's credits. "Maybe you know him."

"Oh really?" Jay-Jay inquired dubiously. Jay-Jay and Cindi glanced at each other. She could only be speaking of one Clarke, seeing how tight the dance circle was in Jamaica.

Cindi refused to believe her. The Clarke whom she knew was levels beyond her own technique. How could he be dancing opposite Joyce?

"What group are you dancing with?"

"Kuji Je Tea Ujana Dance Ensemble. That means 'pride in youth,'" she recited.

"Oh. Ethnic," Cindi concluded as if to invalidate the ensemble.

"I hear they're really good," Jay-Jay replied.

"The show is the Saturday after next at Rochdale. It will be in all the papers," Joyce boasted.

Cindi and Jay-Jay flashed Cheshire grins. They wouldn't miss it for Hollywood.

✖ Twelve

In his side vision she moved like a cloud—gingerly, gracefully. Something was different. He wanted to look at her dancing. She was most beautiful of all when she danced. He carried one glimpse of her with him as far as it could stretch, and let it drift out of the window along with the rhythms he pounded.

"I don't care! Do it the way I choreographed it!" Hassan ordered Clarke, placing his hands under Joyce's thigh. "Try it."

Reluctantly, Clarke attempted to lift Joyce onto his shoulders. "She's not lifting," he tattled.

"You have to lift, dear," Hassan instructed her. "Stay on your center and pull up in here," Hassan said, pulling up on her torso. "That's it, but keep those shoulders down. Help him pick you up. You're sitting your weight on him. Think up."

Up like Merryl, she thought. Joyce imitated her classmate. *No wonder dancers have their noses in the air,* she thought.

"Yes! But you're making it look too hard. This is dance. We can't let the audience know it's hard," Hassan explained.

"She's heavy," Clarke complained indignantly.

"You're weak," she snapped.

"I don't want to hear it," Hassan overruled. "Scott can pick this up in one rehearsal, and female dancers are a dime a dozen. So I suggest you get it together. Show is Saturday." Hassan walked away from Joyce and Clarke.

"A dime a dozen," Joyce said.

"Just one rehearsal," Clarke mimicked.

They laughed.

"How much ballet have you had?" Clarke inquired.

"I'm taking a class now. Outsida that, not much," she admitted with attitude apparent.

He nodded conclusively.

"I'll start you off with a few basic lifts, then we'll try this one again," he said, taking on the tone of a patient instructor. He shook his head wearily. "This is hardly a lift for someone who hasn't had the basics of partnering. No offense," he offered. "But I'm not going to let you injure me because you don't know how to lift. I *need* my back."

Well dig this fruit cup. "I need my back."

"Plié in first and relevé. Every time you relevé, take the weight from your thighs to your hips, your stomach, your chest, and then up to the top of your head," he instructed while illustrating the points on her body. "Loosen up, girl," he added nonchalantly. "I don't want anything from you."

They'd been over the combination at least twelve times. Clarke insisted on repeating it before moving on, although his manner said "forget it."

She knew what was on his mind. He had an attitude about dancing with her because she could move better. Yeah. He didn't like her and was going to be a royal pain the whole way through. You know how those homos carry on. And talk about jealous.

Why couldn't Hassan train her? Why couldn't she dance with Scott? At least Scott put the same feeling into it that she did. Why did Hassan let Clarke get loud with her in front of everybody?

Clarke critiqued her movement with no enthusiasm or judgment, this time. Just the occasional sigh, which she translated as boredom. He would rather dance with a white girl. There was nothing she could do for him. Intensity turned him off. Simplicity made him demanding. Whenever she approached the turns or a series of arm gestures, she could see pain in his face. He didn't want to dance with her.

They were two completely different movers. She was inclined to the downbeat, letting her head go and accenting everything in sharp, deliberate stabs. He was propelled by the upswing, moving swiftly, with clarity and awareness.

Why did she have to think about everything before she did it? Why couldn't she just let it pour from within? *After all, ain't that why we dancing?* To that Clarke said she had to be be fluent in the language before she had license to speak. "Speak plain, Jane," she'd mutter.

"I don't like that," he snapped, imitating her gesture. "It doesn't look right. A good dancer paces his energy. You're using it up before you get there."

"I'm just doing it the way Hassan taught me," she whined, a sound even she detested. Hassan looked up upon hearing his name and resumed his work with the women's chorus, seeing it was the usual squabble.

Clarke could care less. "The arms are supposed to be more flowing, subtle. This is a samba type feeling that we're trying to convey, not funga. You kids think African dance is just one thing."

She sucked her teeth. "You're calling *me* kid?"

He paid her no mind. "Child, I really don't like what you're doing. You're supposed to be a queen, not some bimbo. And we just can't have you doing who knows what, when I'm dancing opposite you with finesse. The audience will pick up on the imbalance right away."

All she could do was let the steam rise to her head and seep through her scalp. Her crinkled hair knotted. She wanted to pop him 'cross his pretty face. She was ready to wolf, "Look, you dilly lily cupcake, you can't really dance, so take a pill and sit down." Instead, it lay thick on her. She just didn't have the tools to fight him without making herself look ugly.

But that was cool. She'd deal with him later. She'd burn him up live on stage. The audience wouldn't even notice him no matter how many pirouettes and croquettes he did. It would be all Joycie.

For the remainder of that rehearsal she danced with her eyes glued to the floor. She looked to J'had, but he was too busy staring out of the window. She looked to Hassan or Tamu for help. They were busy. Her concerns were trivial. Yet the other girls in the studio took ample notice and were gossiping steadily about the leading man and lady and how they could dance her part with their eyes closed and one leg broken, and how she's just trying to show off and how she just better keep quiet and do what Clarke says. I mean, she ain't no Donna Wood.

Joyce finally got a few minutes with Tamu as they dressed. "What is his problem? I wish he would just leave me alone."

"Clarke is serious about what he's doing, whereas you're just here for the fun of it," Tamu retorted, sympathetic to Clarke.

"So you think I'm just here for fun?" Joyce felt betrayed.

99

"You act like it," Tamu informed her in bold print. "Sure, African dance is fun, but rehearsals are always professional. Always. You can't pout every time Clarke says something to you. You'll be pouting 'til next year."

Joyce rolled her eyes.

"Take advantage of dancing with someone as good as Clarke. There's no better experience, that is, if you're serious."

"I'm serious."

"Then act like it. The trick to handling him is to know your stuff. He wants you to shine because he's going to. Clarke moves like lightning when you throw him out in the spotlight. Loves him some applause."

Witnesses nodded and umhmmed in the background.

"You have to be as good and as confident as he is. You should be the focal point of the piece. Your nose has to be in the air, your chest expanded, and the rest of you has to say Queen of the Motherland."

"How can I do that with everyone pointing at me saying, 'she think she cute.'"

Tamu could wring Joyce's neck. How do you get through to someone who won't look in the mirror and see that it's all there?

"I heard the other girls talking and they—"

"They wouldn't be talking about you unless you were any good. That's the way it goes. Studio jealousy. It makes them pull together and bust out their parts. You just have to keep on dancing and pay that no mind. Professionals thrive on spotlight. How do you think ballet dancers get over? If you don't believe it in your head and in your heart, the audience won't believe it, no matter what the rest of your body is doing."

Joyce let the sermon bounce off her ears as she fussed with her scarf. *Tamu don't understand.*

"So when are you submitting to Islam?"

"Today."

Tamu was taken by surprise. "I want to be happy for you," she said, "but do you understand what you're doing? It's not the easiest route in the world. I mean, you can forget about dance."

Joyce said nothing.

"Are you doing it for Islam or for J'had?"

"Both," she answered. "I won't be giving up dance. I'll just do what J'had does. I'll dance and think Islam at the same time. That way my thoughts will be pure and righteous."

Except for the word *hopeless* scrawled all over her face, Tamu was absolutely speechless. That combination of love, ignorance, and hardheadedness wouldn't respond to anything.

"Besides, once I start wearing the Muslim dress, people won't be staring at my behind or cussin' me out in the streets 'cause I don't tell them my name. They'll look at me differently."

So that's it, Tamu summed up in a nod. "Joyce, people will see you as you want to be seen, when you start to look at yourself. You don't have to change your lifestyle to command respect. Just a few things. And I can tell by the way you carry yourself that—"

"I have to go." Joyce cut her off. "I know what I'm doing."

He was soaked from waiting in the rain.

"Are you ready to submit?" he asked, prepared if she had changed her mind.

"Yes," she answered, filled with ideas of submission and J'had.

Lightning cracked across the sky. The rain and the mid-December chill made her long for her leather coat, sitting underneath her bed. Even more, she ached to feel his arm around her shoulder, just to know what his touch was like. It was worth doing the Muslim pledge. They could touch and she could be his lady.

And what would Minnie have to say about that? Nothing. She had no say. J'had would tell Mama his intentions to marry Joyce and Minnie would have *stupid* all over her face. And just when Minnie thought she knew so much Joyce could tell her, "See, Mama, someone *does* want me."

Instead of letting up, the rain became angry, pelting them in rapid fire. Joyce's scarf was drenched. It made no sense to have it on, but she knew J'had would disapprove of her exposed hair.

"We'll wait in here until it stops raining," J'had said, inspecting the inside of the condemned laundromat.

She entered behind him. A hole where one of the planks was missing from the boarded-up window brought air and light to the damp, musty room.

He was so near, and she couldn't understand why they couldn't touch. Touching was something missing from her girlhood. There was no daddy's knee to bounce on. Aunt Em never hugged her, and Minnie was always gone. Then when Mama gave up dance to raise her, Minnie told her daughter that she was too big for all of that "come-to-Mommy" nonsense. And now there was J'had who could look inside of her deeply, with a promise of something warm within him.

His eyes were lowered in prayer when she turned to him.

"J'had."

He looked up, surprised that she had broken the silence.

"What do you feel when you drum?"

Her question caught him off guard. He slid his hands into his pockets as though he were a boy hiding something from Mama.

"Hmmmm?" Her throaty hum had a warming effect and he momentarily lost his thoughts.

"Nothing."

Why couldn't they just love each other? It wasn't like she wanted to hurt him or change him. She just wanted him to love her.

"Don't it give you a feeling?" she asked, hoping to wear down his Muslim defenses.

He said no.

She saw it. His love for her. She saw it and she knew she could move him any way she wanted to. She had him.

"It gives me a feeling. I close my eyes and let it happen. Like that first time I heard your drums and followed the sound to the studio. I wasn't scared 'cause I knew you'd be there," she poured out in one breath.

He just kept staring through the hole in the boards at the raindrops ricocheting like bullets off the streets. He isolated drops as they hit the surface, giving them his most complicated rhythms. That was his only defense against her, his only way to keep her in the background.

"J'had, don't you want me?"

The rain, he thought.

"J'had," she whispered, her lips almost touching his ear.

He avoided the eyes that begged for too much. When they walked, he would gaze into the darkness or above her head. Here, he could not put off the brown, insistent eyes, searching him for honesty.

"J'had, don't you want me close to you?"

"No."

"Don't you?"

"Joyce, please don't."

Her nearness was more than he had imagined from those stolen glances of her dancing in the studio. The

103

power of wanting her was too great. His heart would surely tear from his chest.

Before she realized her first kiss was about to happen, she had already pressed her lips to his and tasted sweet milk. He tried to push her away, but his hands lost their will, falling to her waist. She wouldn't relax her arms about his shoulders until she felt him wanting her.

"How could it be wrong?" she whispered in between their kisses, trying to chase away the taboos in his head. And she pushed her weight down on his shoulders until they sat on the damp floor. She opened her coat and brought his hands to her breasts. She didn't know how sensitive her body was until he touched her and made her love thoughts come true. Every touch became reasons to unlock herself. Give herself. There was more to loving than touching and she wanted to know of it. All of it. She tried to find his zipper underneath his clothes, but he pushed her hand away. He said "No. I'll hurt you."

The thought of pain was inconceivable to Joyce, and she couldn't understand why he wouldn't make her his woman when she was so ready.

"Say you want me," she begged.

He did, over and over.

Joyce could feel his heart coming through his chest with the intensity of his percussion. Or was it her own heart? She held onto him as he began to hold her and squeeze her until there was no Joyce.

The rain continued to pour.

They remained paralyzed within each other's embrace like inanimate subjects of a still life. There was peace in all of the love that Joyce had ever known.

His hand eased its grip on hers. A warm tear fell from his face. He wouldn't look at her. "I'm sorry," he said.

She searched his face, trying to grasp the unexpected apology and the tear. *Sorry* was all she heard. *Sorry.* Something was wrong with being in each other's arms. Something that couldn't be righted for J'had.

Not knowing what to do, she cradled his head in her skirt, and drew soothing circles around his face. The tears continued to fall.

"Everything's all right."

He just kept saying that he was sorry. Then he tore away from her fingers, leaving his crocheted cap in her lap, the star and crescent turned inside out. Touched by death or the devil, one, he shot out of the condemned laundromat as though running could save him before it was too late.

She sat up, stunned. She ran to the door. There was no trace of him in either direction. She called him and called him until his name became nothing but hysterical screams locked inside her. No one heard her in the downpour.

In her stupor, she became lost in her own neighborhood. She was a girl walking around in the rain. Nothing moved her. Not the car that splashed her down. Not the one that slowed to offer her a ride. No. And have them talk to her and disturb what was both dream and nightmare? She could still smell him, feel him touching her, making her warm, making her loved. She couldn't let anything come between her and her only brush with true love.

Minnie had been perched up in the window and came running down the stairs with a bath towel when she saw the girl on the block.

"Well fool, don't you look all silly, all wet up from the rain." Minnie laughed heartily at the girl who didn't know if she was here nor there. And after she fussed over her with the towel she saw that she couldn't get her daughter's face dry for all the fast-falling tears.

"Joycie girl, what's wrong with you?" she demanded, shaking her to make her talk.

"Mmmmmm-mma ma," she bleated, "he was loving me and then he run away. He just up and run away."

Mama hugged her daughter and brought her upstairs. Mama fussed over her and bathed her in vinegar water and made tea and threw her quilt over her and shook her head and said "Lord" over and over.

"Mama, he run away."

"I know, baby," Minnie told her daughter who had fallen asleep, "they all run away."

✤ Thirteen

Joyce could hear Mama crooning about "singing the blues and payin' your dues." Except Mama kept throwing in "payin' your daughter's dues." Whatever. Finally the tune went down the steps and out the door. Gone to work.

In the meanwhile, Joyce sat on the radiator staring out the window. Her arms were wrapped tightly around her middle, her fingers cupped in prayer. Nothing brought back the warmth that she felt with J'had. Her prayer resounded over and over. "If I'm pregnant he'll come back to me and we'll be together. Amen."

In her most intense daydreams she made pictures of their little family, and she was quite sure that she would have a boy. (Girls are too much trouble.) She would let J'had name it one of those Muslim names, talk Muslim, and go to Muslim Sunday school. And J'had would be so proud and would brag to the fellas, "Don't me and Joyce make a pretty baby?" And he would adore her even more because she had his baby. So she just *had* to be pregnant.

Joyce would drift back and forth from sleep to full

consciousness, sitting on the steaming radiator, waking up sore and empty. Empty. Deep down she knew better, even with all of her wishing. Even if she prayed hard enough, a baby wouldn't come from her and J'had's kissing and hugging. That only worked on the late show.

God don't answer prayers, she told herself, unfolding her hands from her belly. Ain't no way a true God would give her love and take it away. Ain't no way a God of any kind would let her hurt so much or make her lonely all the time.

And J'had? He was no different from anyone else on the street. Just a different rap. A respect rap. A love rap. A self-improvement rap. A behavior rap.

Ha ha. Joke on him. He wasn't really slick. He could have gotten over without a rap.

Wednesday they rehearsed without a drummer.

Thursday rehearsal began promptly at four. Joyce took her place in the front line with Tamu, Clarke, and Scott, while Hassan banged on a cowbell in between the rows.

Friday was the last rehearsal before the show, and everyone's nerves were fragile. Insults flew left and right. Two girls dropped out at the last minute. A warrior pulled a hamstring. Half of the costumes were missing. The other half needed drastic alterations. There was no one to work the lighting for the show. The Marley floor had not arrived at the center and there was talk of going without it.

Hassan remained calm. Nothing penetrated his composure. Not dancers with swelled egos or severe stage fright. Not the disappearance of his drummer. Not the discord between his principal dancers.

The panic didn't move Joyce. She floated through the

exercises as though her senses had been anesthetized and only her physical being cooperated.

Any minute J'had would come running up the stairs panting and apologizing to the class for keeping them waiting while he prayed before sundown. Any minute.

At five-fifteen an older drummer came in with a conga and a gourd instrument. He waved to Hassan and sat in the corner where J'had usually sat. There was a paternal friendliness in his burgundy lips and brown eyes that won him an immediate acceptance among the dancers. In his earth-toned dashiki, his tasseled fez, his shades, and his TRANE LIVES button pinned to his shoulder bag, he came across as the seasoned jazz musician.

He toyed with the rhythm. He spoke to the class directly and could make a girl giggle with his call and response, pat-pat-ta-tum-tum-yeh. Where J'had spoke one or two languages, the older man knew ten or twelve. Had he listened to the seventeen-year-old he would have smiled, nodded, and said, "Another punk. Give him a year and he'll be into something else."

At six-fifteen Clarke dropped Joyce from his shoulders, backside splat on the floor. Her mind wasn't on dancing and he wouldn't stand for any of her nonsense. She might ruin his back.

She was determined to keep them all locked outside of her pain. As she picked herself up for the count of eight, Hassan exclaimed from across the studio, "That's right, Joyce! If you fall, use it!"

That was when Clarke threw his hands up and decided that he had had enough of her zombie state. For once he wished she would dance as she usually did—wild and devoid of form. At least she was being sincere. The show was tomorrow. He wasn't putting up with this. Who did she think she was?

He grabbed her and pulled her aside.

"Woman, are you high?"

"Are you?" She gave him apathetic eyes.

"You better check your damn problem at the door." He dropped the theatre articulation like an anchor. "We all have problems."

"Pleeeeeease," she blew in his face, wanting a confrontation.

He walked away. He didn't need it.

Rehearsal ended. She wanted to go home. No one understood the pain that she was going through. They could care less, as long as she did whatever they wanted. Did they care that she was suffering? Well, at least Mama cared. Mama was treating her only daughter awfully well—but Mama thought a baby might be coming.

Tamu interrupted Joyce's daydream to get to the sink. Tamu didn't live too far from J'had. She had to know where he was.

"Have you seen him?"

Tamu propped her black fedora on her head three different ways before answering.

"Um hm."

"When?"

"Yesterday."

Tamu's curt replies made Joyce uncomfortable.

"Where was he? Did he say anything about me?"

"You can find him in Liberty Park. He hangs out with the home boys doing who knows."

Joyce couldn't picture J'had just hanging out and asked Tamu if she was sure.

"He's my cuz. I know him when I see him." She then turned around to meet Joyce's face. "And his name is Malcolm. He's no longer J'had."

There was nothing to say. All of Joyce's righteous

110

swellings of hurt and hostility had been pierced by Tamu. Joyce couldn't deal with the climate and pretended to fix her scarf.

Tamu stared at the self-absorbed girl wondering if Joyce understood anything at all.

"Don't tell me. You're hurt, right? And we're all supposed to feel sorry for you. Isn't that right?"

Joyce turned away. Tamu snatched her back, daring her to cry, pout, or speak. Tamu told Joyce she had stayed up with J'had all night, talking to him, holding him while he cried, telling him to believe.

"But *he* left me."

"Dig, mama's girl. He didn't take anything that you didn't give. Or should I say throw. It didn't matter to you then. Why does it matter now?"

Joyce sank her head. Through puddled eyes, Tamu blurred to a dark figure pointing at her.

"But he hurt me."

"You both the bleeding victims. Love did you wrong. You'll cry. Get over it. Mama done bought you a leather coat and some new dude will walk you home. But doll, he's missing something inside that 'sorry' can't put back. You can't replace a way of life with a girlfriend, or a basketball, or a leather coat." She paused with an inside chuckle. "But you can't understand that, can you? It's moving too fast for you, isn't it, mama's girl?"

"I didn't want to change him. I just wanted him to love me."

Tamu's boots clicked hard, leaving the girl on a bench with her head buried in her arms.

"Well you got it. Deal with it."

"I'm sorry." Her husky sobs echoed J'had's last words. "I'm sorry."

But he couldn't hear her. No one could hear her. It was too late to go to the park and tell him. Some stranger with J'had's face might stare her dead in her face licking his lips, talking about "Yo, Stuff." Some dude from another life might dog her in the streets and get loud with her and tell his home boys, "Check out the Easy A" when they saw her coming.

She couldn't go to the park. No. She had to go home. Mama was waiting for her.

She looked for Terri, Lynda, and Gayle. The block was empty. It was just as well. She couldn't let her girls see her crying. Not her home girls. After all, she was the oldest of the crew.

Ever since Gayle had started to show, Lynda and Terri's moms started keeping them in the house. All of a sudden Gayle's name wasn't good enough to step on.

But did Gayle care? Nay, baby. At fourteen, and eight months pregnant, Gayle was content to resemble a Biafran child with a bloated belly. She didn't need anybody's good word because her little boy was gonna be pretty and named José Emanuel Cortez after his daddy.

The smell of roast meat, greens, and wild rice trickled up Joyce's nose as she climbed the steps. Mama hadn't cooked like that after coming home from work in a good while. The rich seasonings began to twist and turn in her empty stomach like forgotten milk. It was hard to think of food with Tamu's angry lips curling up at her and accusing her of stealing something from J'had. Something that she didn't know she had.

She searched for a vacant place inside herself, small enough to crawl into. A place to hide from ugly.

Joyce managed a faint "Hi, Ma," and closed the door behind her.

Mama picked up on the troubled tone. Her eyes followed the halfhearted girl to the bathroom, and she tried to dismiss it. She heard the water running longer than usual, undisturbed by moving hands. Mama didn't knock. When she opened the bathroom door she found Joyce staring absently into the running water. Minnie moved the girl aside and turned off the water.

She pregnant.

"What's wrong with you, girl?" Minnie demanded, shaking her.

"Nothing."

"Then snap out of it, baby," she told her, wrapping a towel around Joyce's hands. "Now say something."

Joyce wouldn't look up.

Minnie couldn't stand it. "Well? Are you going to tell me what's going on now, or will we have to see a doctor later?"

Joyce shook her head. "For what? I'm not pregnant."

"Fool, it only takes one time."

"We didn't do nothing."

"What? All this time I been worried for nothing." She could barely reconcile the relief with the anger.

"I wanted him to but he didn't want me." Joyce started crying.

"Are you crazy, girl?" Mama's lips trembled long after she finished screaming.

"I just needed him so bad, Mama. I needed him to love me."

"You have love right here, baby," Minnie said. "Don't I feed you? Put a roof over your head? Scrimp and put up with trash on the job so you can go to any college you want? That's all for you."

"You don't love me," Joyce threw back at her. "You don't even want me around. You said I ruined your life."

Minnie threw her hands up. "I didn't mean it, baby."

Joyce didn't hear her.

"No one ever love me. Only J'had."

"No, baby doll. Don't try it."

"If you loved me you wouldn't have left me with Aunt Em all those years. That crazy old witch. Making me feel 'shamed of my tail and making me get down on my knees and pray every time a man looked at me. You wouldn't have left me with her if you loved me."

Minnie could only look at Joyce and see herself at sixteen. Except, Joyce wasn't as hardheaded—and for that she was grateful. Em warned it would all catch up to her. All of her wisecracking and sneaking around and acting grown. So she was paying through her daughter who was capable at age ten of cooking, cleaning, getting a man to look twice, and making babies. What mother wouldn't be frightened of all that?

"I needed time to grow up." Minnie pulled out a cigarette from her pocket and propped it between her lips. "And maybe if I wasn't in such a hurry things wouldn't be this way. Maybe if I didn't think I was so smart I'd have a better life, and so would you. But you couldn't tell me two words back then. I knew it all."

"Things ain't the same like when you was my age," Joyce countered, turning her mother off. *That was then.*

"What's different? I needed loving. But all I had was Em, and she was crazy as a loon. Not crazy-crazy. Just Bible struck. So Eddie gave me all the so-called love I needed. And there I was giving up a precious part of me to some jive high-school dude who didn't know what gold he had. Didn't know and didn't want to know. I cried every night."

Joyce couldn't see her mama crying over no one.

"Wasted my life away, crying over him while he's living the good life with his honey-dipped wife in Cambria Heights. And trying to play it off like we was just high-school pen pals." Minnie laughed at herself. "You couldn't tell me nothing back then. Not a damn thing. He was the only one in the world who loved me and he was gonna come back for me and the baby."

Joyce remained silent.

"See what chasing love will get you. Think of how I felt. Crying over him x years, giving him my heart and my girlhood, and I was just an easy thing to him. You think I listened to Em? She didn't know how I felt. She couldn't possibly know. After all, I was the one who needed love."

"Really, Mommy. What could Aunt Em know about love and being young?"

Minnie sat on the edge of the bathtub watching the smoke from her cigarette swirl. It was still vivid to her.

"Ma," Joyce prodded.

"Hush. I'll tell you," she said. "I was a young girl. 'Bout twelve when it happened, so I had to fill in all the pieces when I got older. And no one talked about it."

"About what?"

"Emmy was about your age. Sixteen. Raising me by herself. Considered pretty much a woman. She was crazy in love with this boy and got in trouble by him. Back then there wasn't all these options you girls have today. Once you was in trouble, you was in trouble."

"You mean Aunt Em was pregnant?" Joyce asked, as though it couldn't possibly be so. Not Aunt Emelia. "Where the baby?"

"The boy laughed at her and went around telling everybody that it wasn't his. Then he started going 'round with other girls, parading them to church and dances in front of her and calling her Sister Collins like he didn't know her. I still remember Emmy crying and carrying on day after day, night after night. But I didn't know what was going on."

"Where's Aunt Em's baby?"

Minnie's eyes were glazed as she remembered the

115

scene of neighbors running over when Emmy let out that wrenching scream.

"Emmy give herself a coat hanger abortion. Ain't been right ever since. All of that screaming. All of that blood. Ain't been right since."

The image of a desperate sixteen-year-old Emelia went through Joyce and left her feeling for Auntie. As though it had never occurred to her before, Auntie became a person.

Joyce and Minnie touched palms at the edge of the tub.

"We always go looking for someone to love us. We forget to love ourselves first," Minnie imparted from her personal scriptures, According to All Mothers.

"But Mama, it be so lonely."

"I know baby. But sometimes, alone is better."

🐾 Fourteen

"That's the problem with colored folks! Don't know how to take care of their own!" Hassan paced up and down ranting about the unswept floor, the filthy bathrooms, and the check that was supposed to be cash. "Had we been some obscure white group from Patchogue, they would have rolled out the royal carpet."

The veteran dancers were used to his preperformance tantrums, knowing that he threw fits like working people needed coffee. While the men unloaded the van, the women set up a makeshift dressing area using a wardrobe rack as a divider. Clarke led a light warm-up, and Hassan straightened out the business of the check. Two younger girls worked in shifts ironing and tagging costumes. One of the mothers did makeup and another braided and beaded hair.

Joyce was steadily dodging Tamu. She rationalized that a confrontation between them would freeze up the dance within her.

Tamu had other things on her mind and didn't notice the pains Joyce took in avoiding her. Tamu was busy coaxing a busty young girl out of her brassiere.

117

"You have nothing to be ashamed of. Be proud. Stand tall. We're Africans today."

After wrinkling her nose the reluctant girl parted with her bra.

Joyce met Tamu's eyes.

"Well?"

"Huh?"

"Well, why aren't you made up yet? We all know you're the Queen of Sheba but even you need makeup, girlfriend."

"I didn't bring any."

Tamu mocked her sheepish reply, letting her know how silly she sounded. "Come. Sit," Tamu commanded as though she could will rain to fall. "We have to do you up right, oh queen of our ancestors."

Joyce sat on the stool totally dumbfounded at Tamu who had erased her anger and disgust from last night. Maybe Tamu peeked and saw Joycie crying inside for J'had and not for herself.

"Now let's match up this skin tone," she chattered while smoothing different powders onto Joyce's wrists, nodding every so often. "A burnt gold should do it."

Tamu finally stopped jabbering. She pursed her lips together, achieving a look of concentration.

Deep inside, Joyce wanted to laugh at herself. Just bust out laughing. The idea of being fussed over made her uncomfortable. And Tamu was no help, laboring over every detail of her face, never flinching or cracking a smile.

No matter how tempted she was, Joyce knew better than to let loose a giggle. It would ruin everything that Tamu had been working hard on these past few weeks. She couldn't disappoint Tamu again. She fought off the laughing fit and kept her head uplifted.

While Tamu sculpted the African deity, another dancer wrapped a red-and-green batik *gelee* around her head. A cloth of the same print was wrapped around her body, pinned twice. The final touch consisted of strings of cowrie shells and bells around the neck, arms, and ankles.

A small group assembled to admire her.

"Feast!" Tamu exclaimed, holding a mirror before Joyce.

Joyce was caught off guard by the woman staring back at her. She, with the regal neck, ripened lips, piercing, brilliant eyes, and pronounced cheekbones signifying a sensual maturity.

Then, all heads snapped toward the men's dressing area. Clarke, inflamed and shrieking like a fool, was ready to strangle one of the boys in the chorus. It seemed that the boy was having second thoughts about going in public half-naked and demanded another costume.

"Look, Miss Thang! Get into it and dance like a man!"

Everyone hollered.

The idea of women dressing did not occur to him. He stuck his head inside the women's dressing area and yelled, "Joyce, I need you!"

She almost didn't know him in his anxiety-ridden state. Some nervous person had stepped into Clarke's body. Joyce was thoroughly tickled and stared at him.

"Let's do the last lift one more time."

She nodded, amused by Clarke's butterflies. *Imagine me helping Clarke.* Although she searched for encouragement, nothing would come out. She didn't know how he would take it.

"Thanks," he said.

She turned. It was too much.

The doors opened to the public and the seats began to fill. The lights dimmed shortly. Joyce watched everything from behind a makeshift wing, awaiting her cue.

Magic began. A kalimba tinkled an introduction and

was accompanied by an elder, whose rich contralto linked the spiritual and the cries of the Congo. From the wings children appeared in number, doing a jumping dance. They formed a circle around the elder, answering her cries with a sweet, lyrical chant.

As the children disappeared, the sounds of gourd instruments and birdcalls were woven into the music. Maidens entered in three rows with baskets of fruit perched on their heads, all held high. Tamu led the magnificent spectrum of multicolored maidens, from the flawless ebonies and earthy cafés to the clay reds and creamy yellows. The bells around their ankles sang joyously as they stamped their feet into the ground.

They exited in threes, all bowing stage right where the men were to enter. The tinkling of the kalimba was overtaken by four drummers in dreadlocks. A thunder rolled off the congas while the warriors paraded their oiled bodies in loincloths. They came at the audience, hurling powerful kicks and firm fists. Scott broke away from the male chorus to solo.

Joyce became so engrossed in the stage magic that Hassan had to eject her from the wings onto the floor when the time came. She jumped in like a wriggling salmon with the drumbeat as her mighty stream. She immediately felt at ease on the stage. It was finally her turn to dance.

The heavy percussion soothed into a slow samba as the nuptial couple neared center stage. The audience responded enthusiastically to their courtship ritual, consisting of subtle hip movements, winding torsos, and floating arms.

Her people had to be out in the crowd. All she heard was "Get it, Joyce!" and "Joy-ceeeee!" And that was music enough. She could burst from the sheer joy of it.

Joyce and Clarke communicated through facial expressions and touch. They were attuned as partners and created an enchantment for anyone who wanted to believe that they were meant to dance only with each other. They each brought their own treasures to the duet. She, the spontaneity and the spell. He, the quickness and control. Man and woman dancing.

In an effortless sweep, the groom perched his bride onto his shoulder. They focused longingly into each other's gaze in a moment of created stage ardor, and he whisked her off into the wings. A low sigh resounded from the audience.

Then the ensemble sprang onto the stage. The nuptial couple returned. The elder showered them with blessings of children, harvest, and old age. To consecrate the earth, the dancers began a vigorous funga. One hundred feet striking the stage sent a tremor throughout the stands.

Without warning, Clarke spun Joyce out into the center of the stage.

And that's when they took her hands and said "come, daughter. Come, child." The women in her back root, with warm and strong hands, broad hips, and loving bosoms. The Ibo and the Mali women, watching down at the Child dancing. Joyce heard the drum within her and stirred a mighty passion of feet and hips and head. And oh! the Child couldn't stop dancing, beyond music, beyond limit. "Leave her be! She touched by the dance!" they mused, spinning her, turning her, smiling down at the Child, who was touched by their spirit.

She whirled and whirled to the sound of some three-hundred–odd home folks and others shouting her name. As the drums halted, the audience roared. The dancers bowed in turn, then in unison.

Joyce was panting, ready to fall out. Clarke held up the dancer who'd danced outside of her body.

"Take a breath and go out there," Clarke urged, yanking her arm. "Bow," he instructed through smiling teeth, and proceeded to pull the disoriented girl in front of the audience.

Her demure bow was rewarded by a flood of applause and the sound of her name. She bowed to Clarke and he reciprocated.

Tamu caught her in an embrace just as Joyce had turned toward the wings. "Go out there and mix."

Joyce searched the stands as though she could spot his face among hundreds of brown dots. Searched hard. Looked everywhere. She thought she might have a sense of his presence drumming for her.

Then Tamu pushed her out toward the people. Minnie's was the first face she saw in the crowd. Minnie's face swelled with pride, and Mama ran to hug her daughter.

"Where'd you learn to dance like that?" she exclaimed, putting her arms around her daughter.

"From you, Mama."

And people she never knew came to her. Telling her how good she was. Where did she study? Wanting to photograph her. Two little girls asked her to autograph their program. Even Clarke surprised her with a warm embrace and told her she was fabulous. And there were Cindi and Jay-Jay and some other kids from the school crowd.

And there he was, smiling at her. Looking just as tall and handsome as ever in his orange-and-blue track jacket. She pretended not to notice him leaning ever so cool and grinning at her and told herself, "Andre you-still-look-good-to-me-Miller."

❧ Fifteen

"Yo! Yo, driver! Wait up!"

The voices from the back of the Special belonged to Melvyn and Marvin. Reluctantly the driver surrendered the door to Joyce, who made it a point to look him in the eye and say thank you. She smiled at the twins, then sat next to Sheilah, knowing they were saving a seat for her. The truth was, she wouldn't know what to say to them for an entire thirty-minute ride.

Life was easier when no one bothered with her, other than to snicker or whisper. Even after the new semester had begun, the attention that she received from the show had barely settled. It was as though her first semester had been rescinded, and she had become part of that group known to seniors and freshmen alike by virtue of her talent. Like the members of the basketball team, the track team, the cheerleaders, and the artists, she was that girl, Joyce, the dancer.

It was all she could do to keep her head up as oncoming schoolmates flagged her down in the hallways with "Hey, Joyce, what's up?" Sometimes she'd pretend to forget her notebook in a previous class, and dart away just to avoid her new friends.

"Hey, lady."

Cindi and Jay-Jay.

"What's up?"

"Glad you asked," Jay-Jay began. "Andre's having a Valentine's gig next Saturday. He said to make sure you got this," Jay-Jay rattled off, handing Joyce an index card penned in red magic marker with two hearts in each corner.

"You *are* coming," Cindi insisted.

"Why not?" Joyce responded, still sifting out their friendliness.

"Bet."

"I hear you've been giving Andre a hard time," Cindi sang.

Joyce stared at her innocently. Over the winter break Andre sent her a Christmas card and a "Thinking of You" New Year's card. Every night she studied the curves of his signature.

"I be busy."

That African royalty was going to her head. You'd think she'd be jumping up and down. It *was* her big chance.

"He wants to get to know you," Jay-Jay said.

"And he's not talking to anyone," Cindi chimed in.

Joyce nodded, determined not to get excited. They could be setting her up for another laugh.

Tuesday was a half day of school. Classes let out at 12:40. Everyone congregated around the intersecting hallways on the main floor, commonly referred to as the Point, to find out where the party was. During the change of classes the Point was the central meeting place to pick up on the latest dirt, the latest steps, and just hang out until the warning bell rang.

All this time Joyce wanted to be included in the parties but never knew about them. Now hooky parties were jumping off left and right and she was always invited.

There he was.

Andre stood out, towering over his group—the 440 relay squad, a few admiring girls, and the requisite clowns that balanced out the cool in every clique. As usual they were trying out a series of jokes about their latest victim, a freshman with superthick lenses and an overbite.

There was no playing it off like she didn't see him. He was staring at her as though his green eyes had summoning power. The laughter died in midair as he strode toward her, slow and assured.

"Hey, lady, what's happening?"

"Not much," she replied, careful not to meet his eyes.

"You're hard to talk to. You never hang out."

"I have rehearsals," she explained, hoping that her thrill wouldn't tell on her. He was close and he was fine.

"Oh," he nodded, feeling the pressure of his crowd on his back. He had to walk away smiling. His rep was on the line. "So what are you doing around one?"

"Cutting out."

"Let's cut out together. We'll leave a little early. Beat the crowd and go to my house. Listen to some music. Talk."

She nodded an "OK." Anything to avoid having something unimpressive come out of her mouth.

"Bet," he told her and sauntered back over to his group like a tomcat who had just copped. "You know that," he bragged as she disappeared down the stairs to the dance studio.

At five minutes to one, Andre waited for her at the top of the stairs. They left through the side door, getting past the hall patrol.

The bus was empty. They sat up front. When their conversation ran thin she looked out the window. She could just as well have been sitting between Melvyn and Marvin, listening to them outdumb each other. Outside of Andre's good looks and his track jacket she didn't know where to start.

"Yo, Sheilah!"

"Yo, yo, Joycie-o!" the girl called back, letting Joyce know that she approved.

"That's my girl," she explained as Sheilah disappeared when the bus pulled off.

Andre nodded, wishing she hadn't called attention to them.

They caught the Q4 to Cambria Heights—Cindi and Jay-Jay's neighborhood. Joyce felt the difference between Cambria Heights and South Jamaica immediately. No projects. No three liquor stores to a block. No four Tabernacle Houses of Prayer to every other block. No boarded storefronts. No rib shacks. No Cadillacs. Instead there were little brown housewives trimming hedges. Sturdy brick cottages stood on green lawns, and midsized sedans boasting college stickers sat along the curbs.

Even when she went to the Deuce, everyone made a big deal out of Cambria Heights. If you lived anywhere near the border, you claimed Cambria Heights over St. Albans, Hollis, or Queens Village.

Andre rang the bell and they got off at 233rd Street. He went into a store and bought a pack of Bambu, then paid for Joyce's potato chips. They walked down 233rd until for no apparent reason Andre got rough, and practically tore her arm from its socket.

"Not down this street," Andre said.

All she saw was two women outside getting their mail.

They were at his house. Two-story, one-family brick with yellow aluminum siding, a large patio, a birdbath, and a colored jockey standing on the front lawn, pointing to a sign that announced THE MILLERS' RESIDENCE.

"No, not through the front," he told her, grabbing her arm once more. He pointed to a side door, instructing her to follow. "My moms would have a fit if she saw you coming through the front. New carpet," he explained.

He clicked on the lights so she could see her way down to the basement. His hands lingered about her waist for the feel of her body. He took her leather coat, appraising it favorably before hanging it up.

She was overwhelmed by Andre's room. It looked more like an apartment than a room, with its paneled lights, wood-grained walls, and carpeting. She couldn't imagine bringing him home to her house. Just look at all this stuff, she thought. Pool table, Ping Pong table, video games, a bar.

"Your room is bad."

"This is the basement. My room's upstairs," he retorted.

"Are those yours?" she inquired, pointing to the drum set. "I didn't know you played the drums."

"Got 'em for my thirteenth birthday." He shrugged. "Don't really touch 'em anymore."

They looked like they'd never been touched at all— just like the minibike resting up against the wall.

Without anything else to focus on, her eyes found photographs and postcards tacked onto the wall. She observed the foreign stamps. "London, England," she read aloud.

"They're from relatives in England. I was born there." His reply was dry, as though he was used to imparting that information.

127

He was joking, she thought.

"Then why don't you talk like they do?" she asked.

"I can if'n when," he retorted in a haughty British accent.

She laughed.

He took a bottle of dark Jamaican rum from the cabinet. She watched him toss ice cubes into two tumblers, filling them halfway with rum.

It was no big thing, she told herself. She had drunk rum a few times with Lynda, Terri, and Gayle. She could handle it. She sipped slowly. She let it sit in her mouth before swallowing. It burned going down her throat. Andre downed the 150 proof like a thirsty man.

He flicked on the radio and motioned her to join him on the sofa.

This was it. He's gonna ask me to go with him. She imagined what his kiss would be like, and the looks on everyone's faces when she showed up in school wearing his varsity track jacket.

"So what albums do you have?" She was going to be cool if it killed her. Make him say all the pretty words.

"You don't want to listen to albums, do you?"

"I thought that's why I came."

He got up, slightly annoyed, and selected an album. He leaned back on the sofa, opening his legs wide.

"I heard a lot about you."

"I heard a lot about you too," she said, wishing she could take it back.

"I saw your show. It was good."

"We're having another show in April at the Billie Holiday Theatre. I won't have a lead like I did in the Kwanzaa celebration, but I—"

"I dig the way you shake that thang," he cut her off, not hearing her at all, and began stroking himself.

Cool just went out the window. Joyce's eyes popped as he unzipped his pants.

128

"Do me," he told her, closing his lids.

Well, damn. He didn't even kiss me. Didn't even say that he liked me. Didn't hold my hand when we was walking. Didn't ask me to go with him. Didn't introduce me to his mama. Didn't give up no decent rap. Just "do me" like I'm some kind of fool.

"Do it," he ordered, drawing his lids open. "You know you want to. Come on."

Well dig this.

Joyce watched his face contort with greed. The face that was oh, so fine. Green eyes, golden skin, and curly hair couldn't mean that much. The more she stared the more obnoxious he seemed. And then just plain old ugly. Why, he didn't look no different than Sam, or any other street dog, for that matter.

That was when she couldn't hold it in and laughed in his face. Even the thought of bringing him home to Mama was ridiculous. Mama would peek his colors the minute he stepped through the door.

"Do yourself. I've got to go," she said smoothly. She got up and took her coat.

"Cut the act. You know you want to."

"What? Me want you? I wouldn't be caught dead with you in public. You ain't nobody."

Joyce went up the steps, heading for the side door. Then she changed her mind. She'd never let anyone say she wasn't good enough for daylight or the front door, she told herself as she walked on the plush rose carpet and opened the front door.

A woman carrying an A&S shopping bag was approaching the walkway, the lawn jockey pointing the way. Joyce greeted her at the front door.

"Who—"

Being smart, Joyce said, "Hello, Mrs. Miller," ever so politely and moved out of her way.

The woman's saffron face turned blue. Joyce left her

paralyzed on the porch. When the door slammed there was all kinds of hot Jamaican screaming and "No, Mamas" wailing from the Miller residence.

Joyce had the last laugh. Not for a bag of potato chips. Not for the privilege of wearing his track jacket. Not to be his woman. Definitely not for Andre Miller.

❧ Sixteen

"Let me hold him. He's so beautiful!"

Gayle had the baby wrapped expertly in blue blankets. She placed him in Joyce's arms. He was a buttermilk-color thing with pink blotches and silky strands peeping out from a blue knitted cap.

Joyce held him close and thought of how she prayed to be full with J'had's child only weeks ago. She laughed at herself for being so stupid and felt a little sad for Gayle, who might never know better.

"What's his name?"

"José Emanuel Cortez, after his daddy. You know José. Runs with Rico and Hombre."

Joyce nodded. *José. Runs with Inez, Yolanda, and Gloria, and make time with his wife.*

"His old lady is too pissed for words 'cause she only had a girl for him." Gayle chuckled.

Joyce saw decay in her friend's front teeth. Minnie said having babies robs your calcium, especially when you're young.

"Did your moms let José in to see his son?"

Gayle sucked her teeth behind that. "He ain't been

'round since José been born. Came to the hospital talkin' some adoption nonsense." Gayle spat. "We don't need him no way. We got money."

Welfare, Joyce concluded.

"So where you two going?"

"We got a doctor's appointment. Moms is a trip. I let her talk me into breastfeeding. Why I do that? Can't go nowhere without him gumming me like we connected for life. Siamese and whatnot. And I only got but this much tit." Gayle snapped her finger. "So I'm getting my milk dried up and he's gonna have to deal with a bottle."

Joyce nodded like her friend made sense. Bottles and babies. Like life on another planet.

"Then Moms telling me some more nonsense about staying inside the house for a month until I close up. Four weeks of this freakin' cryin' and changing these here diapers. I am ready to break loose." Gayle's neck jerked from side to side in disgust as she talked, like it was the baby's fault she felt trapped. Joyce just nodded, checking her out, and smiled at the toy baby in blue and white blankets.

"So where you going?" Gayle asked.

"Rehearsal."

"Yeah, girl. We was diggin' you at that Kwanzaa thing. Me and Terri and Lynda was up there screaming 'Do it, Joy-ceeee!' Did you hear us? We was making so much noise that the people started lookin' at us like we crazy! We ain't cared. We said, 'Yo, that's the home girl. Southside Crew.'" Gayle was proud. "I'm gonna get into some African dance as soon as I get a sitter."

"Um hm," Joyce went along.

"Yeah, I can see myself now, Queen of the Pygmies," Gayle continued, hoping to get Joyce's approval. "Oh, here go my cab." She took the baby from Joyce's arms.

Joyce ran all the way to the studio relieved that she *could* run free. Nothing to keep her down but her dance bag that banged into her side as she trotted. Holding little José was nice, but giving him back to Gayle was all right too. Hassan said she danced like a shooting spark that day. Joyce just knew she was dancing without a care in the world.

Light hadn't caught up with the day when she left her house for school the next morning. She liked it that way. Strolling lazily and enjoying the chill against her face. After all of those prayers for babies to love or a boyfriend to love her she found no greater peace than being alone with her thoughts. That was when she worked out her dances. Alone and in touch. When she felt like it, she'd speak aloud to feel those thoughts. Sometimes she'd answer her own questions with Mama's wit, J'had's caution, or Aunt Em's righteousness.

Knowing about Em had opened her heart for a sad auntie who was still living alone in Hollis, going to church six days a week, and swearing off all pleasures. She tried to picture Auntie twenty years ago, afraid and desperate. And although she wanted to comfort her, nothing compassionate would come to mind. Only Mama seemed to know how to fuss with Em and make her feel loved.

It wasn't quite seven o'clock when she passed the condemned laundromat now being made into a fish fry place. New windows had been installed and the outside whitewashed, leaving no trace of graffiti artists Byrd or Motion. Wouldn't it be strange to order a fish sandwich in the very spot where she felt J'had loving her?

She boarded the bus, relieved that the only other passengers were two women in nurses' uniforms on their way to Queens General. She pulled out her copy of *Slaughterhouse Five* with two chapters due for English. Just before opening it, her eyes inadvertently wandered across the street to a boy waiting for the N6.

He wore gray cotton trousers, a navy pea coat, leather gloves, and he had an Adelphi University bag dangling from his shoulder. He was reading a thick text and hadn't noticed anything coming or going that wasn't in his book.

The driver swung the doors shut and shifted gears. It was him. It was J'had.

The bus began to roll. Her fingers trembled in between the pages. She felt the tiny cords suspending her heart popping one by one, her heart falling.

The bus pulled up to the corner.

The cry of his name was stuck in the pit of her throat. Something prevented her from looking at him. Just as she was naked to him in her dancewear, he was naked to her without his Muslim clothes. She had only known one J'had, and no one else. She couldn't bring herself to look and dropped her tear on page 86, just before the bus swung by. Very quietly, Joyce let go of the handsome young man waiting for the N6.

When she got to school she had no other choice but to hold her head up when she spotted the group huddled in the core of the Point—Cindi and Jay-Jay, Andre, and his track buddies. Sheilah was there, lacing up her high tops. Walking over and waiting for Sheilah to finish would mean eternal suffering while Andre pointed her out to his audience. There was no crowd to blend into and no one to suddenly divert her attention along the way. She heard her name from within the clique as well as the hyena cackling that followed.

Cindi and Jay-Jay saw her coming first, and nudged Andre. Everyone grinned with the anticipation of a showdown.

Joyce blocked out the others, getting a good look at Andre, letting him know that he was no threat, and she didn't feel like shrinking because the Lord of Ladies and Track and Field might wolf her. Her eyes filled with the Andre Miller she knew yesterday, lying back on the sofa, looking ever so pitiful. It was as clear as day—seeing him turn to jelly when she told him she wouldn't be caught dead with him in public. And just as she relived the funniest part, where Mrs. Miller came home unexpectedly, she said a cool "hello" to them and was down the stairs before they could reply.

Cindi and Jay-Jay barely gave the girl a chance to get undressed before they ran down to the lockers to confront her with Andre's story. They found her pensively eyeing her reflection, smoothing out her lip gloss. Joyce pretended not to notice them and tossed her head about in a thoughtful self-inspection.

Cindi nudged Jay-Jay to begin the interrogation.

"We heard all about what happened yesterday," Jay-Jay blurted out eagerly.

"And if we knew Andre was going to be like that, we would have warned you," the other added.

"Of course we didn't believe him when he said it was you who wanted to get down," Jay-Jay offered.

"And all that other stuff about how you threw yourself all over him," Cindi contributed.

Joyce yawned where she was supposed to get excited. "So that's his story," she sighed. "Anything to save his rep."

"Well, Joyce, we all know how much you like him," Jay-Jay said.

"And that you'd do anything to get him."

"To get *him*?" Joyce laughed. "He's not the prize. *I'm* the prize."

"Well *excuse* me," they chorused.

Dig them, Joyce thought, taking a good look at Cindi

135

and Jay-Jay. This time her heart didn't race, wondering what they thought of her and whether she was finally "in." It didn't matter, and neither did they. Joyce clicked her lock, said "later," and went up to the studio. She found her ally, Sheilah, hunched over her knees in the fourth row.

"Hey, Joycie. What was that showdown scene about?" Sheilah asked.

"Nothing really," Joyce stated proudly. "But you know how it is when the man's rep is on the line. Gotta tell that lie." They had to slap hands on that. "But I'm not even concerned."

"Heard that."

When the class was sufficiently full, Ms. Sobol cleared her throat and whipped out her attendance book.

"Just a reminder,"—she paused, taking a quick inventory of her class—"audition for the modern dance festival will be in two weeks. The program will include one of my own compositions—which I will dance with you."

Enthusiasm buzzed around the studio at the prospect of another show.

"The program will include *Shakers* from our Humphrey-Weidman studies, one scene from Ailey's *Revelations* for our Horton studies, and as a special treat I will audition a soloist to open the show with Martha Graham's *Letter to the World.*"

Joyce couldn't help but take in the enthusiasm that ignited around the room as the teacher listed the repertoire. Except for *Revelations,* the titles were foreign to her. It was just as well. She refused to get excited over the modern dance showcase, and wouldn't give Sobol the satisfaction of telling her that her butt was too big for her precious modern dance. Joyce had her own rehearsals to think about. She would be dancing in a theater, not some jive high-school auditorium.

But Joyce had to admit that modern dance wasn't all bad. It was even fun! A lot better than classical technique, and it gave her body room to play. It was dancing from the inside. She didn't mind being on the floor so much, and at least she could move her pelvis and torso. It wasn't too corny. She could put up with it for a semester. And now she had something to contribute when Clarke and Tamu traded Graham combinations.

"Everyone please focus up front while Merryl demonstrates."

Merryl assumed the position, lying with her back on the floor, and waited for the counts. Joyce danced it in her head, blocking out Ms. Sobol's detailed instructions. She often found the step-by-step guidance annoying and wondered how people could learn to dance like that. Why couldn't they just feel it and do it?

"Yes, that's the idea," the teacher remarked. "Now swivel to the left side and focus to finish."

The class attempted the exercise. Ms. Sobol weaved in and out of the rows like a gardener, weeding out the lack of shape and energy.

"Stop!" she told the pianist. "Stop!" she cried, startling the class. "In the blue tights." She looked in her attendance book. "Joyce."

Well, damn! Here we go again.

"Come up front and demonstrate for the class," Ann Sobol beckoned the girl, and then asked Merryl to move over.

Joyce sat in Merryl's spot, front row, center.

"Now, dear," the teacher said warmly, "show them."

Joyce blocked out the teacher's words and trusted the pianist to lay the way. She pulled shape out of her very being as though she could extend both inside and out-

137

side and beyond her physical limitations. She carved her contractions out of love not being made all the way, babies not being born, and Mama's testimony of girlhood gone by. She delivered each phrase with clarity and continuity, transforming the twists and inclinations into the dance she knew.

Within the brief applause she heard a hushed "ohhhh," as though she touched something deep inside someone.

"Yes! Yes!" Sobol praised her. "This is what I've been trying to say—the line, the resistance, the natural pull and release of the contraction. This"—she beamed righteously—"is dance." She smiled at Joyce. The one in the blue tights. "Stay right there, dear."

Joyce didn't see Merryl on the side or Cindi and Jay-Jay to her back. Her focus remained in the mirror, at something wonderful opening up before her eyes.

ABOUT THE AUTHOR

Rita Williams-Garcia grew up in Seaside, California, and Jamaica, New York. After college she pursued a career as a dancer. She is the author of three novels for young adults: *Blue Tights*, *Fast Talk on a Slow Track*, and, most recently, the Coretta Scott King Honor Book *Like Sisters on the Homefront*. She lives in New York with her husband and their two children.